DETECTING
METAL

stories by

Fred Bonnie

Livingston Press
at
The University of West Alabama

ISBN 0-942979-53-2, paperback
ISBN 0-942979-54-0, library binding

Library of Congress Catalogue # 98-73125

All Rights Reserved.

This is a work of fiction. Any resemblance to living or dead characters is a coincidence.

Acknowledgements:
"Feeding the Innocents" appeared in *Aura*
"Those are the Terms" appeared in *Pacific Review*
"The Snake Handlers" appeared in *Wascana Review*
"Birthday Money," "The Friends of Trees," "The Chains of Comand" and
"On the Postcard Road" (published as "A Hearse for the Living")
        appeared in *Fiddlehead*
"Detecting Metal" appeared in *Oktoberfest*
"Detecting Metal," "Feeding the Innocents" and "Rest Areas" received
awards from the Morris Hackney Literary Competition, for which the
author expresses his gratitude.

Typesetting and layout: Joe Taylor
Cover design: Joe Taylor, Stephanie Parnell & Jill Wallace
Proofreading: Lee Holland, Jill Wallace, & Stephanie Parnell,

"Specializing in offbeat & Southern literature"
Livingston Press
The University of West Alabama
Livingston, AL 35470

Notes of Appreciation:

Thanks to Edie Clark, Dilshad Engineer, Michael Macklem, Mark Melnicove, Randall Williams, Joe Taylor, Martin Tucker, Roger Ploude, Joe O'Donnell, Kent Thompson, Colin Sargent, John Staton, and Randy Blythe for publishing my work over the years; to Alan Rinzler and Ashley Gordon for trying to fix it; Fred Hill for trying to peddle it. Thanks also to Logue, Buddy, Ellen, BJ, Susan, Wendy, Doc, Straf, Kay, Merita, Yonjoo, and Jean-Claude for reading it and egging me on. Thanks to my writing teachers, Bill Clark, John Yount, Alan Broughton, Jesse Hill Ford, Allen Wier, George Wolfe, Sandy Huss, Lex Williford, and Tom Rabbitt. Thanks to Abe for telling me I didn't have a theme and to Logue for telling me I did: "Your theme is . . . is . . . . the randomness of life."

Thanks for the energizing and affirmative reviews from Erskine Caldwell, Fannie Flagg, Ray Olson, Mark Childress, Jason Sherman, Kim Underwood, Jane Fox, C. Dino Minni, Sandy Phippen, Alison Demming, Susan Duncan, Bill Caton, Susan Swagler, and Nicki Leone. Thanks to Lyman Wood John Logue, Gary McCalla, John Floyd, and Les Adama for hammering me into a professional writer; to Joy Phillips, Ernie Haynes, Bill Dement, Alexander Mettler, Bev Head and Chuck Bohon for all the work over the alst 25 years. And to Albert Murray for letting us us all know that it's all right to be derivative.

Also by Fred Bonnie:

Squatter's Rights (1979)
Displaced Persons (1983)
Too Hot and Other Maine Stories (1987)
Wide Load (1987)
Food Fights (1997)

Detecting Metal

for Rhonda Lou

Table of Contents

FEEDING THE INNOCENTS

for J.F. Powers

I was once father to forty babies. I was thirteen at the time, theoretically aware of the basics of procreation, but unconvinced that people actually committed such a vile act, even in the noble goal of perpetuating the human species. The prissy girls in my eighth grade class certainly didn't exude any species-perpetuating awareness, but on those evenings when Sister Lilian and I stood in the doorway of the orphanage nursery surveying all the cribs just before we flipped the light switch and a soothing ultraviolet tint fell over the sleep-bound babies in their cribs, I began to sense exactly how the species survived, and my role as after-school daddy to the babies felt, at moments, vaguely erotic.

The only problem was that Sister Lilian couldn't be the mother—she was a nun. I'd grown up thinking that nuns came prefabricated from some nun factory, probably in Massachusetts, and that they were distributed about the state of Maine pre-aged at about fifty. I assumed that the factory did not bother to install species-propagating equipment on its products. Nevertheless, Sister Lilian was the youngest nun I'd ever seen, and she was the first nun I ever found beautiful, although that judgement was based on nothing more than a startlingly warm smile in what was probably a very ordinary face. I came to think of her as my own age, more or less, and my assessment of her as terrifyingly and yet comfortingly beautiful was based, as I said, on her smile, the deft movements of her hands as she changed a diaper or negotiated a spoonful of peach mush into a baby's evasive mouth, the light-stepping, boyish swagger in the way she walked—and what little of her eyebrows and chin her stiff white habit pinched out for the world to see.

During the day as I sat through classes, I wondered if Sister Lilian would eventually turn out as ugly as Sister Geraldine, our teacher, in her old age. Sister Geraldine was the oldest nun in the school, over seventy, very kindly but also a bit senile. Her face was pale and cracked and seemed to have been pulled forward by the eruption of her enormous nose. The eighth grade boys, not a group noted for kindness, had nicknamed her "The Beak." She treated us like second-graders by reading to us a good portion of

the day. She had difficulty hearing and seeing, so she always held
the book up in front of her fading gray eyes, blocking her vision
of the room. The boys would be out of their seats, duckwalking
up and down the aisles to poke and punch each other and generally disrupt everyone's attention. Not that anyone listened to what
The Beak was reading; the girls loved to watch us, which spurred
us on. We could tell by The Beak's inflections exactly when she
was about to lower the book to look at us, and the boys in the
aisles would take to the nearest empty seat. The Beak never caught
anyone, so the clowning went on until Sister Jude, the principal,
happened to stop by the door and peer through the window. Sister Jude blew into the room, her habit puffed with rage, and began herding boys out of the classroom and down the hall to her
office. Sister Jude was a hard, unsmiling woman—her nickname
was The Hatchet—and she proceeded to whack everyone on the
knuckles with a splintered bamboo cane she kept conspicuously
in her office for meting out punishment to those she called *bad
actors*, as if we were all in some second-rate play.

I, inexplicably, was once again spared the rod. My perfect
record for avoiding a whacking remained intact. When the other
boys had been sent back to class, The Hatchet made me stay.

"Francis, I hope you're ashamed of yourself."

"Yes, Sister."

"I don't think you're ashamed enough. After school, I want
you to go up to the orphanage and help the sisters with their work."

"Yes, Sister."

It was a light sentence but also a heavy one. I had avoided a
whacking, but the guys would razz me for the rest of the year
over being sent to the orphanage as punishment. Only girls got
sent to the orphanage.

Holy Innocents was a large, brick mansion that a wealthy Portland family had given to the Church. Three nuns ran the orphanage. The administrator was somewhere between fifty and ninety,
it was hard to say. Trying to guess the age of a nun was like trying
to guess the age of a tree; they were either young or they were old,
and at that point I'd never seen a young one. The second nun was
the cook. She was at least as old as the administrator, and she had
been my second grade teacher some years before. She didn't seem
to recognize me, though.

The third nun was Sister Lilian. She was the one in charge of
the babies. She came into the room as I was bagging up the kitchen
trash. I heard her voice before I got a glimpse of her. I thought she
was one of the girls from school. The other nuns wore black hab-
its, but Sister Lilian wore a white habit, against which her eye-

brows were thick and dark. Because the rest of her was so completely covered, her entire personality seemed crammed into her dark brown eyes and the slight pout of her lips, which seemed always on the verge of a smile. When I looked at her, she did something no female that I could recall had ever done; she gave me a quick but complete survey, from rubber boots to mussed-up hair. She stood no more than three feet away, and I realized that she was also the first grown woman I'd ever seen who was my height or possibly shorter.

"Hi," she said, her eyebrows arching with what I thought at the time was skepticism. I'd never heard a nun say hi. It was always, *Good morning, Francis.*

"Are you the one Sister Jude sent over to help?"

"Yes, Sister."

"Good. I have a lot of trash upstairs. Come on up and I'll show you where it is."

She turned and started out of the kitchen, but I couldn't make my feet follow. My breathing stopped, my neck and face were burning, and my vision was blurred. In a moment she came back to the doorway and stood smiling at me. Her black brows knitted, and her quick eyes picked me over again.

"I take it you're the shy type?"

I said nothing. In a moment she came over to me, took my arm, and led me out of the kitchen and up the stairs. She didn't release my arm until we were upstairs, and I felt her gentle fingers lodged just under my armpit for the next three days. She led me into a large, windowed, thickly carpeted room that was a babble of babies and toddlers. Some were in playpens, some were in walkers, and some sat on the floor amid plastic alphabet blocks, rubber balls, and every stuffed animal ever made. Most of the children who were playing with toys were trying to eat them.

"These are my babies," Sister Lilian announced with a sweep of her arm. The room fell kid-by-kid to silence as the babies turned our way. They regarded me with the reverence that small children bestow upon zoo animals. I saw in Sister Lilian's smile a great satisfaction.

"What's your name?"

"Francis. . . ."

"Is that what your friends call you?"

"No, Sister. They call me *Doof*."

"Hmmm. I think I like *Francis* better. Children, this is Francis. Can you say hello to him?"

The noise level began to rise as the babies gradually turned back to their play, and Sister Lilian took my arm again and led me to a small room with a bassinet and a vast, padded table with three tall stacks of clean diapers.

"There," she pointed, then turned and left.

It took me several moments to recover. I touched my arm where Sister Lilian had twice grasped it, and I recalled the way she had looked at me in the kitchen. I reminded myself to empty the plastic trash container beside the bassinet.

Once I was back downstairs, Sister Delphine, the cook, directed me through a dishwashing session, and I didn't see Sister Lilian again that day. Sister Delphine limped around the kitchen stirring a pot of stew, dumping flour and other things from cannisters into a large metal bowl, and transferring one-gallon cans of creamed corn and stewed tomatoes from one cabinet to another. When she took a sheet of turnovers out of the oven, the room filled with a warm, cinnamon scent. I had finished the dishes, and Sister Delphine sat me down to a hot apple turnover and a glass of milk. All the while I was in the kitchen, I listened for some sound of Sister Lilian from upstairs, but I heard only squalling babies. Sister Delphine prattled on and on about the ice on the back porch and how the milkman almost fell down the steps that morning. But all I could think about was the way my arm felt when Sister Lilian held onto it.

The sound of flapping fabric came down the hallway, and Sister Denise, the administrator, waddled into the kitchen. "Have you finished your chores?"

"Yes, Sister."

"Then you may go on home. Behave yourself and you won't have to come back. Now, take a turnover home to your mother."

*****

By the end of the week I knew I was in love. I was also mortally ashamed of myself for falling in love with a nun. I imagined her in regular clothes with long, black, flowing hair that tumbled over her shoulders and down her back. I pictured myself a few years older, blazing down the highway with the convertible top down and Sister Lilian's hair billowing, and her laugh singing above the hum of the tires. We were always driving along a cliffside road overlooking the ocean as I masterfully guided the car around every terrifying curve.

Each morning as I awoke to my mother's call from downstairs, I tried to cling to my vanishing dreams like someone trying to stuff steam back into a boiling teakettle. And every morning I resigned myself once again to the drudgery of life with The Beak, The Hatchet, The Bird (the second grade nun who talked in a sing-song voice as if everything were a nursery rhyme), The Broom (code name for The Witch, the sixth grade nun), and a bunch of silly eighth grade girls who wouldn't have known the first thing about how to let their hair blow wildly in a speeding sports car. And then there were the guys. To my amazement, not one of them had any wise-ass remarks about my being sent to the orphanage instead of being whacked with the bamboo cane the week before.

On Friday during afternoon recess, The Hatchet came out into the yard and called to me. "Bring this envelope to Sister Denise. Do it right now." She handed me the envelope and gave me a small shove. I tried to act dour and reluctant in front of the guys, but as soon as I was out of their sight, I broke into a run. I even plotted my strategy for having to go back after school that afternoon.

Sister Denise met me at the door. I handed her the envelope.

"Do you need the trash emptied?" I asked.

"No, we're fine. You can run along back to school."

I sensed that the door was about to close. "Can I use the boys' room, Sister?"

She almost smiled. "We don't have a *boys'* room, young man, but you're welcome to use the *bathroom* if you need to. It's right at the top of the stairs."

Perfect, I thought; I'd get to see her after all. I climbed the stairs and looked around for a bathroom. I didn't hear Sister Lilian come up behind me.

"Lost?"

At the sight of her, I could barely speak. "Bathroom," I managed to grunt.

She nodded. "Right there." She gave my arm a quick, tight squeeze just above the elbow. "I'd stay and chat, but I've got to get back to my babies."

I watched her breeze down the hallway, her habit full with hurry, and disappear into the nursery. The squalling of the babies ended abruptly, and I imagined that merely upon entering the room she instantly ensnared them all in her magical, angelic spell.

I went into the bathroom only long enough to leave my scarf on the floor, then I headed back to school, taking my time. I was in my seat no more than five minutes when The Hatchet poked her head in the door.

"Don't stand," she said to the class. "Excuse me, Sister," she said to The Beak. Then to me, "Francis, you left your scarf at the orphanage."

"Oh. I didn't . . ."

"You children need to be more careful with your things. Your parents work hard to buy clothes for you."

"Yes, Sister," I said.

Sitting in class that afternoon I felt like a fish crammed into a glass of water, then set in sight of the ocean. I was so distracted that even The Beak, who never noticed anyone daydreaming, got angry at me and sent me to The Hatchet's office. I was furious with myself. I knew that the penalty would probably be to stay after school and clean erasers. I was right. Four o'clock came, then four-thirty. I'd cleaned every eraser and washed every blackboard in the school when The Hatchet finally let me go. It was already dark as I ran up the street to Holy Innocents.

Sister Delphine opened the door, enshrouded in the aroma of baking bread.

"Here for your scarf?"

"Yes, Sister."

"Do you have just a moment? Can you carry this milk upstairs to Sister Lilian? She's trying to feed the babies and I have to watch this bread."

"Yes, Sister."

I felt remarkable energy in my legs as I climbed the stairs, carrying a gallon jug of milk in each hand. Sister Lilian was just coming down the hallway when she saw me. Her habit was spattered with baby food, which somehow made her seem more appealing than ever when she smiled at me.

"Aha. My boyfriend. I was just coming downstairs for that milk." She took the two jugs and started back toward the nursery. "Thanks," she called.

"Do you need any help?"

She stopped and turned toward me. "Sure, if you want to. Trudy and Barbara had to leave early, so I'm all alone." She turned toward the nursery again, and I followed. "Trudy and Barbara are in your class, I guess. . . ."

"Yeah."

"They're both gorgeous, don't you think?"

"I suppose."

Some of the babies were there only during the day, and many had already been picked up by their parents. Sister Lilian had put the remaining ones in high chairs and arranged them in a half-circle. They all quieted to stare at me when I walked into the room. Sister turned on a small portable radio to a call-in request station where Paul Anka sang about puppy love.

"A little mood music," she winked.

The babies' high chairs were arranged in a horseshoe, and Sister went from one food-smeared mouth to the next, giving each a spoonful of baby food from the small bowls that sat on a card table, just out of their reach.

"You know anything about babies?" she asked.

The question struck me as a bit suggestive, as if she were asking if I knew how they were made. "No."

She winked at me again. "There's nothing to it. You can feed the ones on that side." I watched her a moment, then picked up a jar of carrot mush and held a spoonful tentatively in front of one baby's face. The baby stared a moment at the spoon, then took a swipe at it. Pureed carrots all over me.

Sister Lilian laughed. "That's Woodrow. He's quick, isn't he?"

Woodrow smiled. He could have dumped the whole jar on me as long as it made Sister Lilian laugh. He was a small red-haired boy with three teeth and wide gums. I had the brief impression that he would turn out to be a criminal with a smile like that.

"Try him again. He lets everyone score once in awhile."

The next spoonful went where it was intended. Following Sister Lilian's lead, I worked my way along the circle, jar by jar, baby by baby, then back the other way. I started catching on to the way you had to fake out some of the babies, zipping the spoon past their flailing hands and into their surprised mouths. Others just opened up and leaned toward you. In no time, all the food from the jars was either in the babies' stomachs or all over their faces and high chair trays.

"That's Janice," Sister Lilian said, a note of sadness in her voice. "I'm not sure the poor thing ever had a real meal before we got her."

And then there was Donna, a babbler whose constant stream of would-be words continued even when she had food in her mouth. And Paul, a chubby-faced kid who always wanted to hold my hand with both of his and help me guide the spoon toward him.

"Paul has a more advanced understanding of the process than the others," Sister said.

We were finished in about fifteen minutes, but I could have gone on all night.

"Well." She glanced at her watch. "Record time. So, do you want to help me put them to bed?"

I wasn't about to leave until I had to. "Sure." In addition to feeling limp with love whenever she looked at me, I realized that I was also starting to feel very comfortable with Sister Lilian. More so than any female I had yet known.

"How old are you?" I asked, feeling bolder as I watched her

sponge the babies' faces clean and change them into pajamas that
I handed her from a basket on the floor.

"Forty-seven," she said.

"No. . . ."

"It's true. But I've lived such a clean life I still look the way I
did when I entered the convent twenty-five years ago."

I didn't immediately disbelieve her, since it really was next to
impossible to guess a nun's age. I felt my enthusiasm for her begin
to ebb, saddened to think of her as almost old enough to be my
grandmother.

"Why do you want to know how old I am?"

"Dunno. Curious, I guess."

"I'm really only twenty," she whispered. "But don't tell the
babies. They'll think I'm too young to be their mother." She
watched me for a reaction. I could only smile. "Want to know
what age I'd *like* to be right now?"

I shrugged. "Sure."

"Eighth grade."

I felt my breathing stop as we stared at each other longer than
ever before. She was the one who freed us, finally, from the grip
she had on my eyes. She informed me that it was time for her to
pray with the other sisters before supper. We went downstairs together and she saw me to the door, thanking me several times for
helping her.

I hovered a few inches above the pavement as I walked the
single block home.

The ice on the bare branches of the trees had the look of cake
frosting, and I realized I wasn't the least bit cold.

It was after seven o'clock when I walked in the door. My
mother was furious.

"Where have you been? I've called everywhere."

"I was at Holy Innocents."

"The orphanage? What were you doing there?"

"Helping the nuns feed the babies and put them to bed."

My mother's fury dissipated in an instant, and her look of
anger became one of astonishment. Her eyebrows rose toward her
graying hair, and the wrinkles around her eyes began to soften.
For a moment, I thought she was going to cry. Then she smiled.

"They didn't send me another turnover, did they?"

*****

The next day I was more distracted than ever, but I forced
myself to watch The Beak instead of looking out the window. I
had formulated a plan and convinced myself that I no longer
needed to create excuses for showing up at Holy Innocents.

Sister Denise answered the door. "Back again. What did you forget this time?"

"Nothing, Sister. I'm just here to help Sister Lilian."

Under the old nun's scrutiny, my guilt bubbled up from the murky swamp of my pubescent infatuation. But then the door opened wide, and Sister Denise moved out of the way to let me in. Her eyes seemed to be trying to understand why a boy of my age would want to take care of babies.

"Well . . . aren't you nice," she said.

I bounded up the stairs and down the hallway to the nursery. There was Sister Lilian, sitting Indian-style on the floor reading to the babies. Every mouth was open and drooling as they watched her. I sat down, trying not to interrupt her, but the babies all stared at me. When she turned, her smile flooded her face.

"Well, hello. Table for one?"

"I'm here to help. If you want me to." I couldn't make myself call her *Sister*.

"Good. Woodrow asked if you were coming back. And so did Paul and Donna. Donna told me she thinks you're cute."

I went numb, then heated to a fever as she smiled and toyed with me. We began the feeding routine, and this time I proceeded with great confidence. I even chattered at them some, as Sister Lilian did.

"They love having a guy here," Sister Lilian said. "It gives the little boys a big brother, and gives the little girls a cute boyfriend to look forward to. It's important for little girls to have a boyfriend, don't you think?"

"Big girls, too," I said, amazed at my boldness.

Sister Lilian's head went back with her laugh. "Yes, that's exactly right." Whenever I happened to glance at her between spoonfuls of food that I managed to land with greater and greater proficiency, I found her watching me.

"What . . .?"

"You're very good at this," she said. "A real pro. I see a great future for you as a baby feeder."

The radio played "Personality" over the babies' slurps.

That night in bed, I was transported to a new fantasy, which had moved beyond the sports car to a small, thatch-roofed cabin overlooking the ocean, where we lived surrounded by all these babies. My guilt about coveting a bride of Christ, as the nuns called themselves, only grew, although at moments I felt a sense of partnership with Him. She was the woman we shared. It was both comforting and terrifying, since I had not yet asked for His permission. And I had not asked it because there was no question in my mind that His answer would be a curt *No!*

My visits to the orphanage became the central event that I spent the day looking forward to. I was surprised at how little flak I was getting from the guys. I guess they either didn't care enough about me to rag me, or maybe they had come up with their own reasons for why I hung out at Holy Innocents. Barbara Simmons and Trudy Day, the two most popular and physically developed girls in our class, worked at the orphanage two afternoons a week. As word about my baby-feeding skills got out, I found more girls watching me during class. And when I caught them they smiled rather than turn away.

But they were nothing. Not even Barbara or Trudy could compare to Sister Lilian for sheer class, let alone looks and humor. My fantasies grew bolder as I imagined Sister Lilian in a bathing suit. At times our cottage on the ocean became a cave on a deserted tropical island. We wore only shreds of animal skins, as did our forty babies.

I became increasingly possessive toward the babies. When the parents came just before suppertime to take away the day-care babies, I felt like a robin whose nest was being robbed. At feeding time, Barbara and Trudy seemed amateurishly afraid that a dollop of pureed pear might get on their white school blouses or navy blue skirts. Despite their silliness, I was getting to know them. And like them. And, at those rare moments when Sister Lilian was in another room, I would even flirt with them. Especially Barbara. But I always felt guilty and unfaithful.

The best part of the evening was after everyone else had left and the babies were all in bed. Sister Lilian would turn out the overhead light, and we'd stand side-by-side in the doorway of the large bedroom surveying the cribs and listening to the sounds of infant sleep. The room was bathed in the dim ultraviolet light that was kept on around the clock to fight germs. At those moments I felt both a profound, gray peace and a red, reckless energy. It was all very confusing, and I enjoyed the fun as much as the fear that being with Sister Lilian instilled in me. I'd noticed that since that first day when she led me by the arm, she had never again laid a finger on me, not even to shake my hand, as she did with some of the parents who left their babies there during the day, or the people who came to survey the babies with the intention of someday adopting one.

She must have detected something in the way I looked at her, and since then she had kept a safe distance between us, except during those few moments at the end of the day when we stood in the doorway looking at the cribs. Then she smiled her satisfied smile and murmured, "my babies."

One evening she turned her hand slightly and took mine in hers. My knuckles rested against her hip, and the firmness of her grasp made me tingle with an electric, hormonal glow. "*Our* babies," she whispered. We stood like that for a long time, our fingers moving slightly now and then to change the shape but not the nature of the embrace, which was at moments tight and smiling as we glanced at each other, and at other moments almost sad as we watched the purple room and the nearly noiseless breathing of the innocence sleeping there.

"Sister!"

The moment collapsed, and Sister Lilian jumped away from me.

"We're waiting for you," Sister Denise announced. There was a sternness in her voice that reminded me of The Hatchet, but much worse.

Her head bowed, Sister Lilian scurried away. I knew my face was brilliant red as Sister Denise stared at me. I could not force myself to look directly at her.

"You may go home now, Francis," she said.

I followed her down the stairs. All the exquisite delight I'd felt a few moments earlier evaporated, and a shiver replaced the warmth as I hurried out the door. Trudging home in the snow that had been mounting all afternoon, I wondered what might happen. I imagined that Sister Denise kept a stick in her office for doling out punishment to Sister Delphine and Sister Lilian when they acted up. I wanted to take Sister Lilian's whacking for her, of course, since I was the one who got her in trouble.

*****

The next morning, I stayed home sick. I didn't even have to fake it; I was so deflated I couldn't move. I assumed that God would visit me with a wrath that made the Great Flood look like a pool party. My mother insisted on staying home with me instead of going to her job at the lawyer's office. At three o'clock, I asked her to call Holy Innocents and tell them I was sick and could not come by to help them that day—and probably the next day as well. I spent the weekend in bed, thinking about Sister Lilian, and Woodrow and Betsy and Donna and Paul. I wondered if Sammy and James had gotten over their colds, and if Barbara and Trudy would get any better at feeding the babies.

When I arrived at school Monday morning, I was told to report to The Hatchet after school. I assumed Sister Denise had told her everything. The Hatchet was at her desk correcting papers when I knocked on her classroom door. Without looking up, she ordered me in and told me to sit. I took a seat at the rear of the room, close to the door.

"Sister Denise is very grateful for all the help you've been giving them," The Hatchet finally said in her grave, Hatchet voice.

I waited in silence for her to continue.

"They tell me you know how to feed, clean, clothe, change, burp, and bed a baby better than any of the girls who work there."

I sensed a softening but kept quiet. She finally looked at me.

"Have you forgotten how to speak, Francis?"

"No, Sister."

She looked back down at her papers and scribbled as she spoke. "We're all very impressed. You've done something special for the sisters, especially Sister Lilian."

Here it comes, I thought. I waited for the axe to fall on my corrupt soul, but the Hatchet just kept scribbling away at her papers.

"I have a little gift for you from the sisters. They said to thank you for all the work, but now they've been assigned another nun, Sister Anthony, to help Sister Lilian. They won't need your help on such a regular basis anymore."

The Hatchet reached under her desk and handed me a gift-wrapped box. I must have stared at it too long. "You may open it," she prodded.

With the first piece of wrapping paper that I tore off, I saw that the box inside contained a basketball and a Saint Dominic's School basketball uniform. The Hatchet watched me for a moment, then looked back at her scribbling.

"Now, I want you to go to the gym after school today, put on that uniform, and join the basketball team. I think basketball will improve your concentration. And that will improve your grades."

"I . . . I'm not very good at basketball, Sister."

"Then you'll be sure to improve. You may go now."

So. I was being punished, after all. I started toward the door, only to be halted once more by the Hatchet's now almost congenial voice.

"The sisters up at the home said they might even come see a game or two if you were on the team."

She was a mind-reader of the first order, I saw. It was as if she had taken a raw nerve in one hand and a sugar bowl in the other. I imagined myself stealing the ball from the opposing team's star player, then racing the length of the court, leaving the floor just short of the foul line, and all five feet two inches of me stuffing the ball through the hoop in a blast of net and backboard that would bring Sister Lilian leaping off her seat in a wild cheer. The fantasy ended quickly because I knew the guys would laugh me off the court, but I was too beaten down to argue with anyone, especially The Hatchet. As soon as basketball season was over, I'd try to find an excuse for weaseling my way back into a few regular chores at the home, now that I sensed that Sister Lilian and I were not to be burned at the stake.

"Now get yourself over there," The Hatchet ordered.

"Yes, Sister."

"And plan on going out for baseball this spring."

"Yes, Sister," I said, once again paralyzed by her ability to invade the most private thoughts.

THE CHAINS OF COMMAND

for John Cheever

*F*rank fired Brenda as soon as she came in to work, but now she wouldn't leave. The transit machines clacked and sputtered as the four other operators encoded the new batch of checks and deposits that had been sent up from the teller cages, and all four operators kept glancing in at Frank and Brenda in Frank's little glassed-in office in the corner as Frank tried to figure out how to get Brenda, who sat dabbing her eyes with Kleenex, to leave. Frank suspected that the crying was an act. He had never found Brenda attractive, but with her almost purplish dyed-black hair pulled out of her barrettes as she fidgeted, and her thick, pale make-up furrowed with tears, Frank thought she looked downright frightening. When she wasn't tugging at her hair, she gripped the wads of Kleenex ever tighter.

It was Frank's first experience at firing someone, and he had concluded that he was not very good at it. This was, after all, his first job out of college. He'd worked for three months as a teller, and now he was supervisor of the transit department. He realized that he'd made a big mistake by trying to give Brenda an explanation for why she was being fired. Explaining was bad enough, but Frank had compounded the error when he lied about why he was firing her. He'd told her the bank didn't need five transit operators and could get by with only four. And to add yet a third mistake, he told her he was acting on orders from his superiors.

The real reason Frank had fired Brenda was her incompetence, but he didn't want to hurt her feelings.

"You can't just up and fire me," she said again. "You know damn good and well you need five operators. And I was just starting to catch on. You just don't like me." She tried to summon a defiant smile, which made her look all the more grotesque. "Well, let me tell you something, Big Guy. You picked the wrong damn person to pick on."

Frank had not counted on an argument. Brenda had always been meek and solicitous, apologetic for her many errors, always polite when she had to ask her four coworkers to help her figure out which check or deposit slip she had encoded wrong, which threw the computer out of balance. Her refusal to accept being fired was the first hint of assertiveness Frank had even seen in her.

"Brenda, why don't you just go ahead home and . . . ?"

"Because I want to speak to someone with some friggin' authority around here. And I ain't leaving until I do. Where's Mr. Polling? He's late for work. Why don't you fire him? I ain't never been late for work."

No, Frank thought. You just kept everybody here late while we all tried to figure out where you screwed up. Twice that week Donna or Pat had had to read back the long computer printout item by item against the stacks of checks and deposit slips to find the items that Brenda had encoded incorrectly. That put everybody behind, which meant that Frank's group ran up more overtime than the rest of the bookkeeping department combined.

He stood up from his desk and opened the door. "I'm sorry about this, Brenda, but someone had to go and you're the newest operator. I think the bank was very generous to give you a week's pay."

Brenda's eyes slipped back to the envelope in her hand, but she did not move. Frank left the transit room to go downstairs, hoping Brenda would be gone by the time he got back. He planned to wait for his boss, Ken Polling, so that he could warn him that he'd bungled Brenda's termination. He figured if he could get to Polling before Brenda did, Polling might understand. After all, it was Frank's first firing.

He knew Polling would come through the employee lounge to get a cup of coffee on his way in, so Frank drew a cup and stationed himself at the table nearest the door. Moments after he sat down, Brenda got off the elevator and came toward him.

"I want to talk to you," she said.

"About what?"

"Why you fired me."

"We've already talked about it. Don't make me fire you all over again."

"Carol says there's *always* been five transit girls."

"Now there are four."

"Yeah. Until you hire somebody else."

"Brenda . . . I wish to hell you'd just go home."

"Don't you swear at me!" She stood by his chair as if he were an errant child and she was going to swat him.

Frank was glad the lounge was empty. "Look, Brenda. I'll make a little deal with you. Go home, calm yourself down, and when you're ready to look for another job, maybe I'll give you a good recommendation, okay?"

"I don't need you recommending me for nothing!"

Frank shrugged. "Okay. Then I won't." He caught himself drumming his fingers on the table and stopped.

Brenda smiled, her dried tears webbed through her make-up. Her air of resolve continued to surprise and worry Frank. "I got connections in this place that you don't even know about," she said. "I could get you fired in a second." She snapped her fingers. "I'm talking about the powers that *be*, Big Guy. Friends in high places, if you know what I mean."

"So, maybe you should go home and gloat in the privacy of your bathroom."

She leaned forward. "You know something? You're a mean, ugly little creep. Them glasses make you look like some little . . . creep."

Frank decided that insulting her might be the only way to get her to leave. "You know, Brenda, if I had a face like yours, I'd be working hard to improve my personality."

Rather than fly into a rage, she coolly sat back in her chair. "That's it. I'm gonna tell them you discriminated against me."

"How so?"

"Cause I ain't as good looking as Donna and Carol and Pat and Stephanie. You think you can push me around just cause I ain't good looking."

Frank began to think it would be unwise for Polling to find him in the lounge with Brenda. He stood up and started toward the elevator, but it was already too late; Polling opened the door.

Polling was a short, muscular former state police officer with a blond crew cut, about forty, Frank guessed. He always looked as if he'd just come from a funeral, and Frank had never seen a single variation in the man's expression. Polling nodded at Frank and went directly to the coffee machine.

Brenda jumped up from the table and followed him. "Mr. Polling. I want to talk to you. I've been discriminated against."

Polling glanced at her then continued toward the elevator with his coffee. Frank had already pressed the call button.

"Well, you can file a complaint with Personnel," Polling said. "Morning, Frank."

The elevator door closed on Brenda, who, to Frank's relief, did not get on.

"I'm glad you didn't say *good* morning," Frank grinned.

"You say that at noon, not at nine."

Frank let his smile last only a moment before he lowered his voice. "I canned her this morning and she's mad."

"You expected her to be happy?"

"I didn't expect her to be anything. She's always been . . . I dunno . . . quiet."

The elevator door opened, and Brenda, who had take the adjacent elevator, was waiting for them. "I want to talk to you in private," Brenda said, her eyes watery again.

Polling glanced at his watch and headed toward his office. "Sure."

Brenda followed. Frank's tight stomach relaxed a little, now that the buck had been passed.

*****

Back in his office, Frank was aware of a slackening in the usually constant clatter of the transit machines. He could feel all four women watching him, but whenever he looked out toward them, they pretended to be working.

"All right, what's the problem?"

The machines were instantly silent. They all glared at him, but Carol, who had short blond hair and wore too much eye liner, was the only one who spoke.

"You didn't have to be so mean to Brenda."

"Mean? What are you talking about? I didn't even tell her she was incurably incompetent."

"She wasn't all *that* bad."

"She was terrible. You were whining about Brenda yesterday. She's had three months, she's kept us all here late at least once every week, she's basically stupid, and now she's gone. You people ought to be thanking me."

Carol picked up a check and started working again. "Brenda said you were mean to her. You didn't have to be mean."

As Frank's gaze passed from Carol to Donna to Stephanie to Pat, each woman began to work again, and the transit room was once again the clackety vibration that Frank liked to feel in his feet. No one looked at him as he went back into his office. He was looking over the balance sheet from the previous evening shift when Brenda came into the transit room and dragged a chair over beside Carol's machine. Frank decided to step in before Brenda got something going. All the machines stopped again as Frank crossed the room.

"Excuse me, but if I remember correctly, you don't work here anymore."

Brenda had redone her makeup and now leveled her dry, hateful eyes at him. "Then don't try to give me orders."

"I think you need to go along home, Brenda."

"I think you ought to try to make me."

"Do I have to call the security guard?"

"You can call the Army Reserve for all I care."

Frank stood his ground. "You happen to be disrupting one of my employees."

Carol glared at him. "We're just talking."

"I see. And does the bank pay you to be a counselor, or a transit operator?"

Carol, who happened to be the best operator and therefore the least fireable, loaded her glare with righteousness. "I'm on break right now."

"Well, if this is a break, do it in the lounge."

Carol and Brenda glanced at each other, then got up and started out of the room. Stephanie, Pat and Donna immediately followed. Frank went back into his office and tried to read the paper but couldn't concentrate. He picked up the phone and called Ken Polling's secretary.

"Hi. This is Frank."

"Sinatra? Oh, I thought you just might call."

"You're too funny. Did Brenda Swanson just talk to Polling?"

"Yes. And with the door closed."

"How long?"

"I dunno. Ten minutes?"

"How did Polling seem after Brenda was in there?"

"Like always. He had me make her an appointment with Mr. Fletcher."

Fletcher was Polling's boss. Good, Frank thought. Polling was going to pass her along, too. Frank told himself that maybe what he had done was exactly what you were supposed to do.

"Thanks."

"Wait . . . something you should know." She lowered her voice. "Ken resigned. Today's his last day. But don't tell anyone I told you."

Frank hung up. If Polling was not going to take the buck he'd been passed, then Frank needed to let Mr. Fletcher know what was going on before Brenda got there. He began to type a note.

> Memorandum
> To: Dirk Fletcher, chief of operations
> From: Frank Riley, transit supervisor
> RE: Disgruntled former employee
> You may hear from a Brenda Swanson this
> morning. I had to fire her and, of course, she
> is not happy with my decision. She may make
> some wild allegations, which I can assure you
> are totally unfounded. I'm sorry if this matter
> causes you any inconvenience.

There. Ass covered. He liked that word, *unfounded*. He'd never before had occasion to use it, but now it struck him as the most profoundly appropriate word in the entire business world. He was sure that his decision to fire Brenda was beyond reproach. He sealed the envelope and carried it upstairs to Mr. Fletcher's office on the top floor, removed from even the vaguest tremor of the operations Mr. Fletcher was said to oversee.

Dora, Mr. Fletcher's secretary, looked accusingly at Frank when he walked in. She was a stern-faced, middle-aged woman who had taught high school business classes for thirty years before coming to work at the bank.

"Could I leave this for Mr. Fletcher?"

"Yes, but he may not be around much this week. He's taking over the marketing department. Very busy."

"Sounds like a promotion. Good for him. By the way, has a Mrs. Brenda Swanson tried to see him this morning?"

Dora didn't even need to glance at her appointment book. "Eleven o'clock. But I doubt if she'll get a chance to see him. I've already arranged to send her to Mr. Sheldon."

Morris Sheldon was the executive vice president, and easily the most hated man in the bank. Good man to pass the buck to, Frank thought. He'd run Brenda off with a single glance. Frank left the letter for Mr. Fletcher anyway, then went back to his office to write a new one to Mr. Sheldon. When Frank got back to the transit room, the women were all at their machines working. No one looked at him.

> Memorandum
> To: Mr. Morris Sheldon, executive vice president
> From: Frank Riley, transit supervisor
> RE: Disgruntled fired employee
> I hate to bother you with mundane details in
> Mr. Fletcher's absence, but one of my transit
> employees, a Mrs. Brenda Swanson, has
> turned out to be very troublesome, so I felt
> obliged to fire her this morning. She seems
> to be suffering from a nervous breakdown and
> holds you directly responsible. I gave her a
> week's pay and let her go, but I thought I
> should warn you that the woman may try to
> see you, and I wanted you to be aware of the
> wild, unfounded allegations she may make.

*****

Frank took his time getting back to his office, feeling as he did like a man in control of a crisis. He stopped in the mail room to tell a few jokes with the janitors; then he went back through the lounge to see if Brenda was still around. She was not.

When he got back to his office, the machines were once again quiet, and the four women were whispering to each other. Frank stopped in the doorway, looking from one to the other, and the machines started up again. He was about to walk on to his office when Carol spoke up.

"Mr. Sheldon called a minute ago mad as hell."

"He sounds mad when he says Merry Christmas. So what?"

"He said for you to call him the second you walked in."

"About Brenda?"

"He didn't say. But I hope that's what he's mad about."

Frank stared at her a moment, then let his eyes drift down the row of machines to Donna and Pat and Stephanie. All four women were in their mid-twenties, all were married and had at least one pre-schooler in day-care.

"Will someone please tell me what's going on? I canned Brenda because I got sick of listening to you people complain about her. All of a sudden, she's some kind of hero. What's up?"

"She's not as stupid as you think," said Pat, a plain woman with drab brown hair but a quick smile and razor wit. "She's trying to work another job at night. She's usually tired when she gets here in the morning."

Donna, a tall, dark-haired beauty with a waist-length pony tail and room-filling smile, pouted now. "She has to take care of her mother, too. She's about ninety."

Stephanie, a freckled redhead who looked no more than sixteen, was the next to defend Brenda. "She only learned to type a couple of years ago. That's why she seems slow on the machine."

Frank looked toward blond Carol, who made a defiant face. "See? I told you you shouldn't have been so mean. . . ."

Frank went into his office and closed the door. He tried to hold onto his feeling of having sashayed out of trouble that morning, but he could see his fingers quivering as he punched the numbers on his phone.

"Sheldon."

"Sir, this is Frank Riley in transit."

"Riley, have I ever met you?"

"No, Sir. I don't think so."

"Then you're in luck. If I knew you well enough to recognize you, I'd come down there and give you a good kick in the ass."

Frank said nothing. He noticed the transit girls watching him and tried to appear unruffled. As a dying man's life flashes before his eyes, Frank's brief career as a banker flashed in his. He'd have to borrow money from someone until he found another job, and that would mean Mildred would get depressed again, as she did the last time he was out of work, maybe need to be hospitalized like last time. And Frank would have to ask his mother to take the kids in until things got back to normal.

"You don't fire someone who has something on you," Sheldon continued. "It's kind of a no-no in the world of corporate tranquility."

"I'm sorry, Sir. I didn't know she had anything on me."

"She says she's got more on you than they had on Nixon."

"I have no idea what. . . ."

"Look, Riley. She's got something on somebody or else she wouldn't be so goddamn sure of herself. Get up here."

Frank hung up and thought a moment. He considered calling Mildred to tell her he was about to be fired, but that seemed like his worst idea in years. At least not until he found out if he was going to get any severance pay. He tried to seem calm as he walked through the transit room.

"If anyone phones, tell them I take calls by appointment only."

"I'll try to remember," Carol said.

Frank went straight to Mr. Sheldon's office. He was surprised to find the office full of people. Polling and Fletcher were there, along with Mr. Sheldon and Winslow Barton, the bank's president.

Polling sat more or less at attention in his chair. Dirk Fletcher, a big, red-faced man with hands like catcher's mitts, sat with his legs crossed and a massive finger extended along his cheek. President Barton, a scholarly looking little man with gray hair and glasses, sat quietly smoking his pipe, studying Brenda's personnel file, which included her photograph. He looked pale, a bit uneasy, Frank thought.

Mr. Sheldon stopped pacing long enough to tell Frank to shut the door. "Now what's going on, Riley?" he demanded.

Frank withered under the stares of so many bosses. "Well . . . I was just trying to fire somebody who doesn't seem to know a check from a dry cleaning ticket."

"Have you been screwing her?"

Frank nearly laughed. "No, Sir."

"She claims you tried."

"In all due respect, Sir, I couldn't . . . I mean, she's not my type."

No one smiled. Sheldon turned toward Polling. "You been nailing her, Ken?"

"No, Sir. I kind of feel the way Riley does."

Sheldon began pacing again. "She claims someone in the bank seduced her. I'm not putting up with anything like that." He stopped in front of Fletcher. "Was it you?"

"Not me. I'm with Riley and Polling. And I haven't even met her."

Sheldon started in again. "Then she's obviously lying because it sure as hell isn't me." He glanced at President Barton and a tiny smile broke. "Unless it's you, Win."

Polling and Fletcher smiled, too, but Frank decided it would be unwise to appear amused. Everyone seemed ready to dismiss the whole thing when President Barton sighed and nodded.

"I'm afraid I'm the guilty party, gentlemen," he said.

Sheldon stopped and turned to stare at President Barton. He held the back of a chair as if he might fall. "Jesus Christ, Win. Tell me you're kidding."

"Well . . . it was at a party a couple of weeks ago," the president explained to the ceiling. "Everyone was drunk. A costume party. I ran into her in a closet—thought it was the bathroom— and she was in there changing. She was naked from the waist down, and she started laughing. . . ." He shrugged. "Hell, it seemed like the thing to do at the time. How was I supposed to know she worked here?"

"Why'd you have to tell her *you* did?" Sheldon asked from inside his hands.

President Barton shrugged again. "We were there in the dark, groping each other, you know, and just whispering nonsense. She told me she worked in a bank and asked me what I did. I told her I worked in a bank, too. It seemed like a big joke, Shell. I swear, I never laughed so hard in my life. We were kind of dancing, humming songs to each other. She was just a ton of fun."

Frank tried to picture the situation. Brenda? Fun? Dancing bottomless in a closet with this otherwise dignified looking executive? A woman who works two jobs to take care of her aged mother? A bank president who likes to have fun?

"The Swanson woman had just gotten divorced," President Barton went on, "and my wife and I have an agreement about these sorts of things. It was indiscreet. I was a bad boy. But you know, she had the sweetest breath. . . ."

Frank let a loud sigh escape, causing Polling and Fletcher to glance his way. Fletcher's white eyes rolled in his red face, and stolid, starched Ken Polling, who still sat at attention, almost grinned.

But not Sheldon, whose smile had turned mildly vicious. "Then maybe you should be the one to handle this thing, Win."

President Barton took the pipe out of his mouth and pointed the stem at Sheldon. "I don't have to handle it, Morris; that's why I have *you* here."

Sheldon grunted and turned to Fletcher. "Find out how much she wants and pay her off," Sheldon said.

"I'm in marketing now." Fletcher squirmed. "I've never laid eyes on this woman. And besides, I'm on a plane to a banking seminar in Boston in less than an hour."

Everyone turned toward Polling, who had sat silently in his chair. "I'm on my way out of here," Polling said. "I don't think I'm the one to fool with it."

Sheldon, who was on his feet pacing again, stopped a few feet away from Frank.

"I already fired her once this morning," Frank said.

Sheldon's glinting eyes seemed to take from Frank's answer the solution he'd been seeking. "Then I guess you're the one who started all the trouble." Sheldon pointed a long, narrow finger into Frank's face "Fix it, young fellow. And fix it goddamn fast."

*****

As if she'd been privy to the meeting upstairs, Brenda was waiting for Frank in his office. He sat down at his desk and took a sip of his cold coffee.

"All right. You can have your job back," he said.

"I changed my mind. I don't want that rotten job."

Frank sighed. "Then why are you here?"

"I want a better job. Or else I'm gonna sue."

"And just who do you plan to name in your suit?"

"Anybody I have to."

"Like who?"

"I don't have to tell you nothing."

Frank began to discern that she was just shooting BB's in the dark. She clearly had no idea whom she'd made it with. "And I don't have to give you a job. Let's face it—you don't have anyone to sue, you have no witnesses to whatever it is you think somebody did to you."

Brenda smiled. "The hell I don't. Once I sue, I'll get the whole damn bank in a lineup. Then I'll know who it is that owes me."

Frank knew it was useless to argue with her. He also saw an opportunity to finally shuffle her along to someone else. "I only have transit jobs," he said. If you want something different, you'll have to talk to Personnel."

Brenda nodded toward the phone. "Get Ken Polling on the line."

Frank picked up the phone and punched Polling's number.

"He cleaned out his desk a few minutes ago," the secretary said. "I *told* you he was leaving."

"He quit," Frank told Brenda. "You want to talk to *his* boss?"

"Damn right."

Frank called Dirk Fletcher. The secretary told Frank that Mr. Fletcher had just left five minutes earlier to catch a plane. Frank hesitated a moment, then dialed Morris Sheldon's office. Mr. Sheldon, it turned out, was out to lunch and would not be back until late that afternoon.

Frank pondered whether he should call President Barton. He knew the president would not understand why Frank was involving him again. Because it's *your fault* this is happening, Frank would tell the president. Clean up your own damned mess.

Brenda, now calm, cold and tearless, watched his every move.

"All right," Frank said. "We'll try Win."

"Who the hell is Win?"

For the first time that day, Frank saw how the land really lay. He leaned back in the chair and watched Brenda as she sat in his. Perhaps she would make a better boss than a worker.

"You don't really know who you were with that night, do you?"

She finally seemed wordless, embarrassed. "Do you?" she asked.

"Yes."

"Tell me."

Frank only smiled.

She mashed out her cigarette in Frank's ashtray, but her motion seemed careful rather than angry. "I want a friggin' lineup," she said.

Frank told her he'd be right back. He went to another office down the hall and called President Barton. "Sir, this is Frank Riley. I hate to bother you with this Brenda Swanson business again, but she says she'll sue if we don't give her a better job. And that she wants to see the bank's senior management in a lineup."

"Oh no. . . ."

"But I think I know how we can get around it, Sir."

"What do you have in mind?"

"Sir, if I can have Ken Polling's job, I'll just give her my own job. That way I'll be able to keep an eye on her and make sure she doesn't try to give you any more trouble."

Barton hesitated only a moment. "Good thinking, Riley. The job's yours. I'm very grateful to you for thinking of that."

Back in Frank's office, Brenda sat in his chair reading his telephone messages.

"Do I ever have a deal for you," Frank said. He paused for a moment, savoring Brenda's satisfied smile, pleased with himself for grasping the intricacies of corporate structure. Ultimately it would be Carol, Pat, Stephanie and Donna, not even the president, who would determine just how long Brenda might last.

BIRTHDAY MONEY

for Bernard Malamud

If I'd a been playing with regular money instead of birthday money, I might coulda won. But when you got to hustle instead of play for real, you get so that holding back on purpose makes you miss the easy ones in a real game when you're trying to play good. But I been hustling college kids for about three months now. I'm glad to get a five-dollar game. And sometimes you think you're hustling some dumb-ass, but it turns out you're playing real competition, a real good shooter that thinks he's hustling *you.*

When you're out of shape, not practicing, drinking too much, and playing with birthday money, you bound to lose.

Marlene don't understand none of that. Here it was her birthday, and I showed up with a goddamn box of candy when I promised her some living room furniture. I didn't tell her I had the money and lost it; I told her I just never did have it. If I could get paid to sweat, I could have made some money that night. I won a few small games and a few beers, but I couldn't get anything big going. Your name and your face travel so fast. Half the time I can't even get a game in Birmingham. I gotta go to Memphis or Jackson or Florida to get anything decent going. And it takes money to travel like that, so you work like hell to save up from the five dollar games so's you can go to Florida and get into the good money games, but Marlene don't like me to go to Florida no more. She don't understand about money, and she don't understand about luck. She thinks if you go out to shoot, you automatically bring back some bread every night. She don't understand luck, not even good luck. So what's she do? End up with a gambler.

"You look so cute leaning over that table like that," she tells me the first night. "I like the way your eyes look when you lean down and line up a shot with that stick."

I get taken in right away, see, because most gals don't pay no attention to a gambler unless he's a high roller. They ain't interested in some poor bastard like me trying to hustle college kids for five bucks.

So she's back at Sammy's Tavern the next night and starts

hanging around me again. I'm still there from the night before, since Sammy let me sleep on some tore-up cardboard cartons in his storage closet. Marlene trots in about six o'clock and hands me this fifty-dollar cue stick. I say, "Thanks, Baby, but I can't use that thing. This is kind of a low profile type of situation. You don't want to attract no attention to yourself."

She acts a little hurt but makes like she understands. She leans close to my ear and says, "You mean, it's dishonest?"

"Kinda, yeah."

She don't come back the next night, and I get to thinking about her and that ruins my concentration. She's small, like me, and kind of wiry looking. Dark, pretty skin and this big old friendly smile. I could see her yakking away at her girl friends whenever she wasn't flirting with me. Nice girl. Clean cut and nice smelling. A secretary, she said. I ain't never even stepped foot in a office, so I ask her what she does. She looks at me like I'm joking and starts trying to explain.

"Well . . . I make copies of things and file things that get lost, and type things, and bitch a lot, and make bad coffee for my boss."

Then she asked me what I did.

"I play pool."

"No . . . I mean for a job."

"I play pool."

I could see this look come into her eye, part suspicious, part admiring. "Like on TV?" she says.

I had to laugh. "Maybe someday. I ain't that good yet."

That made her smile again. It was okay to be a pool bum as long as I might be on TV doing it someday. "You're very modest," she said. "I love that in a man."

That was that. From then on, Marlene and me was in love. No questions asked. Not for awhile anyway.

*****

While we're standing there getting all horny over each other's eyes, this cat name Blake I been hearing about for over a year or more comes strutting in, looks around the place, spots me and comes over. He was a big ole bear of a dude, thick hair half way down his back, big ole beard, sunglasses. He had four friends with him, and they all looked pretty much the same. It was like Blake wouldn't let you hang out with him unless you looked just like him.

Anyway, I knew Blake, but I didn't know he knew me.

"You Tony?"

"Yeah. You Blake?"

"Yeah. You wanna shoot?"

I had fifty, sixty bucks in my pocket. I didn't want to get into a big game unless I had four, five hundred. But I didn't want Marlene to think I was chickenshit either.

"Yeah. I'll play. Twenty-five a game?"

He kind of smirks, like he's doing me a big favor just to play. "Sure," he says.

I lost the flip and racked the balls. I was nervous as hell. I seen him play once, and Blake was a good shooter. Maybe the best around. He was a big bastard, too, and I could see he was the kind that only smiled when you told him somebody died or lost his arm or something. He wore a leather vest and had these big old rounded shoulders and looked like he could lift up a car.

So he breaks, and he's got a stroke like a bulldozer on meth. Them balls run all over that table like they was terrified. Four stripes and a solid in on the break. So he's got 'em all down in about a minute, and I'm racking again. Another sledge hammer break, another run, and I'm racking a third time.

Marlene leans over and whispers in my ear. "Is he any good?"

"He's great."

"I thought so."

Five racks later, I finally get a shot. I'm thinking, damn—I'm paying twenty-five bucks a rack to watch this ape play pool. It wouldn'a been so scary if I'd a had the bread, but I could feel the sweat drooling down the back of my skivies, and that ain't no help to a man's concentration. But I made the first shot and left myself in good shape, then I ran three racks on him. Marlene was real impressed. She was leaning on me and there was something sweet about them drinks on her breath.

I finally missed. It was a bad time to miss. When you got your foot on a dude's neck, you can't let up. This time he ran six racks before I got a shot. There was a big crowd watching now, including Blake's friends, who all looked real serious behind them shades. I'm starting to think I won't get out of there alive.

"Listen, sweetheart. You got a car?" I whispered to Marlene.

She caught right on and whispered back. "Yeah."

"If this gets bad, we might have to leave in a hurry."

"But I have to give my girl friends a ride."

"You can come back and get 'em."

"God, this is exciting."

Hearing the way she said that made me feel real depressed. I told myself that next day I'd go back to painting houses again. Anything to get out of living like this.

Blake missed and he was standing there staring at me, waiting on me to shoot. He said something to one of his buddies, and the guy started out the door. I figured Blake was sending him out to watch the parking lot in case I tried to run.

I don't like to fight. I'm fast, and I'm rugged, and I used to could fight pretty good for my size, but I'm thirty-seven now. I don't like to fight no more. And the last time I had to fight, I got my ass kicked bad enough to make me think twice before starting some shit with anybody. Two broke ribs, big old scar on my bald spot.

"Your shot, ace."

I missed. It was an easy shot, too, but I was thinking shape instead of shot and I missed. Blake ran two more racks before I got another shot. I couldn't even remember how much I owed him. While I was watching him shoot, I see Marlene looking at me with all this sympathy.

"You don't have money to pay him, do you?" she whispers.

"How'd you guess?"

"Cause you look so sad." She leaned real close, and her breath in my ear gave me the chill bumps all over. "I got some money, in case you need it. So, you just play. And beat him."

A chick will make you feel lucky sometimes. I started feeling a whole bunch luckier, knowing I wasn't going to die that night if I lost. I ran four racks, then when Blake got another shot, he scratched on the eight ball. Things went straight to hell for him. He lost the next nine racks and all of a sudden I was into *his* wallet. I could see it in his face. A naturally mean bastard will look even meaner when he starts losing.

"Look, man. I gotta head out in a while," I told him. I thought he might raise some kind of hell, but he looked kind of relieved.

"Sure man. Anything you say."

"How bout one last game for a hundred?"

He got this smile, and I knew I'd made another enemy.

"Hey, man, I'm dumb but I ain't stupid." He threw what he owed me on the table, jammed his cue stick in the rack, and started toward the door. I knew better than to rub it in by saying something like, "Thank you." His buddies stood there and stared even after Blake was out the door. I added it up in my head before I even touched the money on the table. I took about a hundred off Blake. Just enough to piss him off.

But I had to feel good, too, because Marlene was planting a big, deep kiss on me, rubbing her hard little titties against my chest, telling me she liked me, whether she loved me or not. And telling me to take her someplace, anyplace, so we could be alone for a few hours, even my car. I didn't have a car just then, but I told her if she'd sit and have a few beers with me for another hour or so, I thought we might be able to get Sammy's storage closet. She laughed and laughed. I decided I liked her, too.

"What about your friends?"

She turned around and put her hands up to her mouth. "Take a cab, Girls," she hollered to them.

*****

You marry a chick who'll do you like Marlene did me that night. I suggested it after about three weeks. We was getting along real good at the time. It was my fourth, her second.

"Will you get another kind of job?" she asks me.

"No."

"Not ever?"

"I doubt it."

"Then we can't get married."

"That's up to you."

"Damn you! I'd get different job if you asked me to."

"Like what?"

"I used to be a dental assistant. I could do that again."

"Be a dentist. Then I can just quit work altogether."

Some guys don't like to have no woman support 'em, but I never have minded that myself. Marlene didn't like the idea, but she bad wanted to get married. She was Greek or Lebanese or something, and them folks don't like for a gal to stay single too long, cause they know she starts putting out whether she's got her a husband or not.

I never did meet her people. Marlene told them about me and how we was getting married, and they said don't bring him around. That was okay with me. I don't know what to do around folks like that. Rich folks that live in big houses. This rich guy named Fairchild that saw me play one time—he made a bunch of money off me on side bets—invited me to a party at his house once. I didn't know what to say to nobody. The only thing saved me was he had a big old pool table, the best I ever played on, and I just shot all night. A guy who was a friend of Fairchild's wanted to play me, and I won almost a thousand bucks off him. But Fairchild comes up when I'm alone getting me another beer. "Don't take his money," he says. "Melburne's just showing off, and he can't afford to lose a thousand bucks. His wife will leave him." I didn't know what the hell to do. I mean, I already spent the money in my head paying off guys who was leaning on me because I owed 'em. I took Melburne's bread anyway. I know Fairchild thought I was a piece of shit for doing it, but I don't know how to turn down money I won fair and square. I ain't never see old Fairchild again.

Marlene's people are rich, so I was glad I didn't have to meet them cause I wouldn'a knowed how to act. We just got married down to the courthouse one Friday at lunchtime, then went down to Gulf Shores for our honeymoon. Back on Monday morning. Marlene went over to her folks' house every Sunday to eat with them, but I never had to go. I knew they was giving her a hard time cause she was always real quiet when she came back to the apartment. But after a couple of hours, she'd be okay again. I just had to make sure I was there when she got back. If I was gone, she'd just lay on the bed in the dark and cry until I got home.

Once in a while, she came around to the bars with me at night. She even seemed to enjoy it, as long as I was winning. It was like she didn't mind what I did so long as she knew where I was at. Most of the time she was just fine. I was bringing home twice as much money as her and she liked that. She got kind of pissy when I lost. Like I said, she don't understand about luck.

She didn't like it when I headed off to Florida the first time, either. But I get a better shot at the money games down there. I can always find a place somewhere around Fort Walton and Panama City where they don't know me. There's a lot of money there and bars just packed with fools drooling to lose some.

"You didn't even ask me if I wanted to come," she says.

"I can't. I'm gonna be with some friends, I already told you that."

"They mean more to you than I do."

"Hell no, hon. I'm going down there so's I can buy you a nicer car and some pretty clothes."

"You better."

That first trip, I made twelve hundred, Sax made four hundred, Eddie made four or five and Billy Bomb made a grand. It ain't a bad idea to travel with a guy like Billy Bomb 'cause he's about Blake's size. He don't like to fight, but he's big enough that most guys don't fool with him. We stayed in one room, flipping to see who got the bed and who slept on the floor or out in the car. And we got the big games, like I knew we would. We had about four good trips like that, and I had about two thousand bucks in the cupboard.

"Why don't you quit and try to get a job, now that you got some money ahead?"

"Sweetheart, you don't quit when you're ahead."

"I'd quit something if you asked *me* to."

"Good. Then quit harping."

"I want to come on the next trip. Just you and me. We'll go in my car and stay somewhere on the beach and have a good time."

It sounded good, so I said yes. But it ain't the same when you go somewheres with your wife. The first night I played, I lost. I was nervous because it was a tough place, and this drunk kept coming on to Marlene just to get my goat while I was playing his buddy. And I couldn't get lucky. That night I tried sleeping on the floor so's I could get the feeling of being there with Billy Bomb and them. Marlene was mad as hell, and the next night she starting flirting with some guy just to get back at me. I lost four hundred. I took her back to the hotel, checked us out, and headed back to Birmingham.

It was the first time I felt like it was a mistake to marry her, but I think a man's gotta live with his mistakes.

"Are you going to get a job now?"

"No."

"Are you going to just keep playing pool?"

"I reckon. It's the only way I know to make a living."

"You don't have to make a living. I'll support you so you can get some training and get a job."

"Training? For what?"

"I don't care. Just as long as it's not pool."

*****

So I signed up for a course in how to repair computers. I knew I wasn't going back for a second day, so I stopped by Sammy's on the way home and ran into a guy who was in the computer class. He recognized me and wanted to know if I played pool. I told him I played some, and we racked 'em up. He was good but he was stupid. He refused to believe I was beating him. I wasn't trying to hustle him or nothing; I didn't hold back, and I was running two, three racks at a time, but he still thought he was going to beat me. I took two hundred dollars, plus his watch and a decent diamond ring. I tried to get him to put up his car, but he smartened up at that point.

Marlene didn't seem mad or nothing when I told her I didn't like the computer class. She said fine, I could just pick something different. But I didn't. I sat around for two or three days, then Marlene told me if I wouldn't pick a new course to study, she'd pick one for me. So she signed me up for a course in how to be a paramedic. It wasn't as boring as the computer course, but it warn't nothing I could see myself doing. I got to talking with this old boy in the class. Sure enough, the subject of pool came up. After class, we went looking for table, and I took a hundred and twenty off him.

Marlene was signing me up for one class after another, and I was getting some poor bastard from the class for anywhere from fifty to two hundred a night. I went to a different class everyday—welder, cook, TV repair man, air conditioning installer, and carpenter. Since I wasn't staying in none of them classes, it wasn't costing nothing, so Marlene kind of left me alone. Meanwhile, I was bringing home all the bread I was making, but I made the mistake of bragging on what I was up to. Hell, I thought it was the best racket I ever come up with. But Marlene flipped out when I told her why I was trying so many classes. She thought I was just trying to figure out what career I wanted to go after.

"By the way," she says with this mean little grin. "Some guy named Blake called a couple hours ago. Left a number. Isn't he the guy you were shooting with that night when I almost had to bail your sorry ass out?"

Oh, yeah. Blake. I don't know how he got my phone number, but I knew we was gonna have to have the number changed. Blake was leaving messages at Sammy's and every other pool hall in town wanting to know when we was gonna play again. I put off calling him back. I won't lie; I was scared of him. I thought I was real lucky that first time. I beat him, but he was better than me and I knew it.

When I quit looking for a course to take so's I could get a real job, Marlene started staying over at her folks' place on Saturday *and* Sunday. I could tell the thing was going to end. I tried to get her to come out with me again and watch me shoot, but that just made her cry.

"I hate those places."

"Well . . . you don't hate that fur coat I bought you last month now, do you?"

"I hate pool."

"Well, sometimes I do, too. Ain't no reason to cry."

"Please quit playing pool. . . ."

The big problem was that somewhere along the line, I started to love this gal. She was the best one I ever had. She was sweet in bed, especially when she was emotional, like after she saw her people. And she did everything she could think of to keep me home. I mean everything. We'd be there at the door and she'd be in a nightie or something. She knew about what time I'd head out, and she'd run and change just to try to keep me there.

"Don't you want me to do a little something to Big Mac before you go?"

"No, cause you'll do it for three hours. . . . Baby, I gotta go."

I was still getting enough games to support me day to day, but I wasn't getting no big games. Not like in Florida. Not even like the games I used to get with the guys in those classes I signed up for. When I told Marlene I was going back to Florida and that she wasn't coming, she said she'd be gone when I got back. I told her that was up to her. I knew her people had a strong hold on her, but I figured mine was stronger.

I called Sax and Billy Bomb and them and set everything up. We planned to leave in two days, on Friday. But Marlene left to go stay at her folks' place, so I called Billy Bomb back and told him we oughta just go ahead and leave right away—drive all night and be in Panama City the next morning.

"Like old times," Billy Bomb said.

"Yeah. Just like that." It made me feel real bad because I never thought the old times was all that great.

*****

Florida didn't work out. It wadn't spring break or summer or nothing like that, so there wadn't many people around. Plus, I kept worrying about Marlene and what her people were telling her about me. You can ignore that stuff if you only hear it once or twice, but when you hear it week after week, it'll get to you. I called home about every hour, but she was never there. I bet I called twenty times in two days, and the phone just rung and rung. Then I got to wondering if she was out with her girlfriends, going around to bars like she used to do.

I was losing every game I played, but I stayed on because Billy Bomb and Sax was winning, and because I kept thinking I'd be okay if I could get her on the phone and tell her I was coming back just as soon as I made a little money.

I finally got ahold of her folks' number and called over to their place.

"Pappas residence. . . ."

"Marlene there?"

I thought he hung up on me or something, but finally Marlene comes on.

"Look, Baby, I'm coming home just as soon as I can get out of here."

"Are you in trouble?"

I remembered that first night, when she thought I was in trouble with Blake. I figured I oughta try to get a little mileage out of that. "Just a little bit, Baby. But I'll be okay. Now you get on home and be there waiting on me, okay Baby?"

"Please don't get hurt."

I could hear her starting to cry, so I got right off. I ate my losses, about eight hundred, and headed home. I felt bad about lying like that, but I figured I had to do something. I figured I might even have to quit playing pool and find a *real* job, as Marlene always put it. She was so glad to see me she never even mentioned finding a job, or taking more classes, or any of it. She was just glad to have me back, and I couldn't bring myself to tell her I was lying to her when I was in Florida. I decided to lie a little more. "There was this cute little ole gal down there in Florida. She was watching me play. Makin' eyes at me . . . man!"

"You didn't talk to her, did you?"

"No. I just thought about you."

She laid back down on me. "You get a star on your forehead."

The next day, I felt so bad about losing half my stash and lying to her, I went out and looked for a job. I looked around at all kinds of places—restaurants, bars, strip joints, taxicab companies—but nobody was hiring. All I could find was day work, unloading trucks, packing bottles of corn syrup in boxes for the train, and I was lucky to get that. The two mornings I went down to the corner where they hire day people at, there was two hundred guys to get twenty-five jobs. Somebody told me the economy was going to hell, and didn't I know unemployment was the worst it had ever been since The Depression? How the hell was I supposed to know? I don't work for nobody, so I don't get laid off, and I don't read no paper.

But I'd been seeing it in the pool halls for a year or more. Like I said, five dollars was good money, even with the college kids. And all the hustlers show up trying to beat each other for a beer or a dollar. Blake's after me all the damn time. I don't even go to Sammy's no more cause I know there's a note there for me from Blake.

Money started getting tight at home. I got on a losing streak that lasted for a month, a dollar at a time. I was making hard shots and missing easy ones, just like the college kids. And I couldn't keep the eight ball on the table. It wouldn't go in on the break, but it went in any other time it could. I scratched so much I thought I had crabs.

And when I ran out of cash, I kept playing anyway, losing the TV, the stereo, the VCR Marlene bought me as a wedding present. I tell her they was screwed up and I brought them to the repair shop. She wants to believe me so bad she don't even argue, even though I can see she knows what's going on.

Meanwhile, Marlene refuses to visit her folks because she don't want to hear them talking about me no more. She finally tells me she lied to them and said I was studying to be a engineer.

"You mean like on a train?"

"No, the kind that builds bridges and banks and stuff."

"What'd you tell 'em that for?"

She looked at me in a way that made me feel awful. She kept on looking at me and I made myself look right back.

"Don't you know?" she says.

She was gone the next day. It was better that way because there was a guy coming to get the couch. I had to bet it in a game and I lost it. I started getting crazy and betting the car, my clothes, the rest of the furniture, everything. I was so crazy I was even smiling when they hauled stuff off. I started drinking what I didn't save to lose at pool, and Marlene stayed away. She came over when I was gone to see how much stuff was still there, and she hauled her own clothes off when she saw mine was gone. When I called her at work, they said she had a new job and they didn't know the number. I called her at her folks' place and whoever I was talking to said they didn't know where she was at, but they thought she was staying at a friend's place.

I was trying to get ahold of her because her birthday was in three days, and I had left a note in the apartment telling her I traded in the old furniture on some new. I guess that got her attention because she showed up that night at Sammy's.

I ain't real emotional, but when I saw her there at Sammy's, I just about broke down. "Baby, you got to come back home."

"Maybe when you get me that new furniture."

"We still got a bed, Baby. That's the place to start when you're talking about furniture."

"You sold all my stuff, didn't you?"

"Bad luck. I swear I'm playing as good as anybody. I can't win because all I can think about is how you left me when I was down. And needed you."

It was just a matter of getting her out of Sammy's then. I had about six dollars and I took her to Waffle House to eat something. She sat on my side of the booth and was real sweet to me. I guess she felt guilty over what I said about her leaving me when I was on hard times.

"Are you gonna quit playing pool?" She said it real sweet, not nagging.

"Yeah. In just a few days."

"Quit right this minute."

"Just give me two or three more days. Look, your birthday's in two days. I'm planning to buy you a whole new set of living room furniture. How's that?"

"You promise?"

"Sure. I'm playing great now. Besides, that other furniture was garbage. You used to complain about it all the time, remember?"

"Yeah. . . ."

She got a lot better after that. We stayed around the Waffle House drinking coffee for a couple of hours, and then she wanted to drive downtown and look in the windows of the furniture stores. We had to go in her car. I lied that mine was in the shop. I knew I was ready to lie about anything if I had to, including the furniture I told her I'd buy her. And she was ready to believe me, just so it would be sweet for us that night.

And it was. The sweetest ever, maybe. Like when you both know it's probably the last time you're gonna have, or might be.

*****

Man, did I ever bust my ass the next day. I unloaded trucks for six hours, and then I played pool for six. I went home with four hundred and seventy-six dollars and forty-one cents—up from sixty-two cents, which was what I had left after all that coffee me and Marlene drunk at the Waffle House the night before. I thought she might spend the night with me, even though she told me the night before she wanted to still stay at Shirley's—she won't tell me who the hell Shirley is or what phone she uses now or where she's working at in her new job or nothing. When I got back to the apartment at ten, the place was dark, not even the stove light on, and there's a notice taped to the door that it's gonna take eighty to get the lights turned back on. And a note from Marlene saying to call her when I got the new TV and stereo and furniture, but not before then.

Next day, I unload trucks for nine hours—sixty-one bucks for that—and shoot pool for eight. I come home with six hundred and fifty, and stick in the coffee cup in the cupboard with the rest. I already priced the furniture out, and I found this one dude that'll sell me everything I need for fourteen hundred this month, seven hundred the month after that. I got one day left, so I don't bother to unload no trucks—just shoot pool all day. By noon, I got fifty-five more bucks. That afternoon I make three hundred and sixty-two more. I call the furniture store and find out they close at six.

I got fifty more bucks to go, and in walks Blake. His three friends kind of gather around me while I'm trying to line up a shot.

"Heard you was here," Blake says. "Thought you might give me a chance to get back some of that you took off me."

I was playing real good, but I didn't want to take no chances. "Can't. Gotta go."

He laughed. "You don't get to go that easy, man."

Sure enough, Blake's friends move in front of the door. I knew I wasn't gonna have no luck. He flipped a big silver dollar, I called heads, and it come up tails. Blake didn't smile or nothing, he just grabbed the first stick he saw and started chalking it up.

"Since I let you call when the game was over last time," he says, "I guess it's my turn tonight, huh partner?"

I pictured that couch in the store window with me laid out on it in a funeral home, but I couldn't tell if the knife sticking out of me was Blake's or Marlene's. Then I seen there was fifty or sixty knifes, and they was all mine.

THOSE ARE THE TERMS

for Flannery O'Connor

As Ginger sat on the hood of her old yellow Chevy in the lumberyard's gravel parking lot, she found herself enjoying the stares of the people in the cars passing by. She'd gotten up early enough to spend an hour choosing, by trial and not a whole lot of error, the right clothes: a white cotton, short-sleeved blouse with puffed shoulders, blue jeans that were tight enough to be sinful on anybody else, and new brown sandals that matched her wide, pure leather belt. She'd also spent a little extra time combing her hair into a full, auburn-gold flow and getting it to hang just right through its blue cotton head band. She was ready by seven, but she found it harder than it had been all week to leave the mirror. She wanted to look as good as she could for Marcus. And if the people now staring at her from the passing cars thought she looked good, then she must have done something right.

Ginger had figured out when she was fourteen that she could get any man she wanted, from young and dumb to older; and even though the older ones still might be dumb, at least most of them had jobs. She'd also decided that whichever man she did finally pick, he was going to have to be a Christian. She'd made that decision two years ago, when she was sixteen and her red hair barely reached her shoulder blades, and her boyish body looked more stretched out than filled out, as her half-brother Bobby-John had told her once when he was being ugly.

Her first real understanding of herself came on a Sunday morning when her mind wandered from the back of the pew in front of her to the preacher's eyes, which lurched with a certain regularity between the church ceiling and the front of Ginger's blouse. She figured out right then that her good looks didn't have anything at all to do with her; God had simply made her good looking so she could attract any man she wanted so she could manufacture a big old brood of new, God-fearing, bill-paying, Crimson Tide Christians. If there was anything in this life she knew she was ready to do, it was to breed some new Christians for God and His greater glory.

She wondered why Marcus was late, and if he was a Christian. He was a nice enough man—she saw that right away when he came into the hardware store where she worked to buy tools for his garden. He'd just bought his first house, he told her. She also thought he was real good looking, slender and a little tanned, with dark hair, bright blue eyes that kind of stared but seemed shy at the same time. Twenty-five, she guessed.

When he asked where he could find some rotten hay to use as mulch on his tomato plants, she offered to help him find some. She had Friday off, since it was The Fourth, so she told him where and at what time to meet her. But so far he was eight minutes late. Maybe Yankees couldn't get up early enough to meet somebody at eight on a holiday, she thought. She knew nothing about Yankees; she'd never been north of Cullman County, but she had a suspicion they probably weren't so different from everybody else. Except for the fact that Marcus said he'd planted beets in his garden. And she'd never heard of a single soul to put rotten hay on his tomatoes.

*****

She was so busy trying to remember if she'd ever seen a picture of a beet—she knew they were red—that she almost didn't notice the dark green pickup that slowed onto the shoulder and glided to a gentle, dustless halt in front of her. Marcus sat staring at her a moment, and Ginger decided that he was even better looking than she remembered him at the hardware store. His hair was a little tousled and his shirt was open a button or two extra.

He leaned his head through his open window. "Hi."

She could tell by the way he looked at her that he thought she was pretty. A warmth spread all over her just beneath her skin. It was a familiar warmth that sometimes pleased her, sometimes frightened her, almost always confused her. Right now it pleased her but also made her instinctively try to conceal her pleasure behind a boyish brusqueness.

"Y'eat breakfast yet?" she asked.

"No. . . . Did you want to eat first?"

She slid off the hood and started toward the driver's side of her car. "Follow me."

Ginger could hardly watch the road. She and Marcus were having a conversation of glances and grins in her rearview mirror, and it made her feel like the one time in her life she'd been drunk. She'd gotten drunk with her half-brother Ollie just so she'd know what it was like, but Ollie had gotten really ugly, talking about her body parts and trying to touch her, and Ginger swore she'd never drink again. The Lord had plainly shown her why she shouldn't.

But she didn't want to think about Ollie or anyone else in her family right then; she wanted to think about Marcus. She loved watching the way the wind in his open window blew his hair over his forehead into his eyes; and every time he brushed it or shook it back, she wished she were doing it for him. She could see the possibility of falling in love with that bit of elbow that stuck out his window.

They were getting to know each other fast, she thought.

"I shall not sin, Lord," she whispered in a laugh. "Unless it is Your holy will." In her head, a chorus rose to the heavens. "Aaaay-*meeeeeeeee*-in!"

*****

Ginger had been fashioning a plan for the past two days. She would feed Marcus first—show him the biscuits she had actually mastered in her final high school class—then take him looking for rotten hay. She pulled into the parking lot of her apartment complex and pointed over her roof to the one empty parking space three or four cars to her right. She saw the opportunity to be modest; she could get up the stairs and unlock the door before he got out of his truck, or she could let him watch her as they mounted the steps single file, her first, since she would have to lead the way.

"This is really nice of you," he said with a smile that was half look, half look-away. "I really need some hay."

"We ain't found you none yet."

Then he was following her up the stairs. She suddenly felt exposed, and she hurried instead of taking her time and sashaying, the way she'd thought she would. Her place was clean, and the plant hanging in the window above the sink seemed more spread out and purpler than ever.

"It smells good in here," Marcus said.

"I don't live in no paper mill." Without even looking, she sensed his smile. She liked the way he smiled, the way he never gawked at her in a sinful way. And if he did, he was too quick for her to catch him. He stood in the living room glancing around at her plants, her guitar, her bulletin board on which she'd pinned two bumper stickers: *Honk if you talked with Jesus today* and *Elvis Lives.*

"I like your apartment," he said.

Ginger had mixed the dough and covered it with waxed paper before she went to meet Marcus, and now she cut it into biscuits with a coffee mug, laid out the biscuits to form a heart, and slid the cookie sheet into the oven. The grits, the instant kind, would take only a minute. All she had to cook now was the ham and eggs.

"You like your coffee strong or weak?" she asked.

"Strong."

"Good. So do I." The cookie sheet clanked as it buckled in the oven's heat. "So, what do you do?"

"About what?" he asked.

"For a living, Silly."

"Teach school."

"Like what?"

"High school English."

"I used to could do good in that." She paused, so she could show him she knew what pauses were for. "But I quit."

"Really? When?"

"Tenth grade. I couldn't stand it no more."

"Stand what?"

"My life." The pause went on longer this time. She set out plates. He looked at her magazines now, and at her one book. It made her nervous. She'd never seen an English teacher anywhere but in school, and she'd never even heard of a young male English teacher. She'd always thought of her teachers as old women from the teacher factories, although that idea occurred to her only now as she led him by the arm from her two years of *Glamour Magazine* to the table.

"You sit here." She brought the bowls of food from the countertop beside the stove to the table.

"You always cook breakfast for strangers?" he asked.

"I don't know. You're the first one."

"Stranger? Or the first one you've ever cooked breakfast for, period?"

She'd cooked breakfast in bed for her momma on that one Mothers Day, a week before she told her momma she couldn't take it anymore and was moving out. Ginger plugged in the coffee maker and decided not to answer. He had already spooned some scrambled eggs onto his plate and seemed uninterested in an answer. She asked him a question of her own, just to make sure he didn't press the breakfast cooking question.

"Why are you an English teacher?"

"I like to read. Now I get paid to do it."

"I don't. Hated it in school." She sat down. He was about to bite into a biscuit and she reached for his hand and stopped him. "Wait."

He looked at her with surprise but said nothing.

She continued to hold his hand after he lowered it to the table. She bowed her head, closed her eyes. "Heavenly Father, thank you for this food, which I hope is cooked okay, and thank you for the glorious weather on my day off. And thank you for sending

Marcus to visit me this morning, and for the birds that are singing, and for the low humidity so's my make-up don't get all messed
up." She considered stopping there, but Marcus's hand was warm,
more callused than she had expected, and she liked the way they
squeezed on each other, just about equally. Something told her
that if he wasn't a Christian yet, she could turn him into one.
And save his eternal soul.

"And thank you for the paycheck you made them give me,
Lord, and for not letting my mother call back again last night or
this morning." She still didn't want to let go of his hand, but she
did want him to taste her biscuits.

"Amen."

*****

During the next few moments Marcus seemed excessively shy,
and Ginger suddenly swam with self-doubt about her cooking.
The morning's warm flush trickled through her cloudy mind
again, and for several moments she could not look at him. She
decided to talk, since she couldn't stand the silence.

"I hated school. Period. Quit the day I turned sixteen and
could do it without asking my parents. Got a job the same day,
stayed with my girlfriend Reba for a month, and then got this
place."

His smile trickled back. "You would have stayed in school if
you'd studied English with me."

She imagined walking into a classroom and getting uneasy like
she did when he looked at her. He was right; she might have stayed
in school, but not to study.

"Hang on a second."

He got up from the table and went downstairs. He was back
before she could sneak to the window to see what he was doing.
He held both hands behind his back and nudged the door shut
with his foot.

"Got something for you. Close your eyes and give me a hand."

But as he curled her fingers around a bunch of stems, she
opened her eyes before they were even really closed. Yellow flowers. Ginger didn't know what kind they were, but she decided
they were the prettiest flowers she'd ever seen.

"They're so preeeeety!"

"From my garden. I was going to give them to you after we
got the hay, but I was afraid they'd wilt in the truck."

No one had ever given Ginger flowers before, and she gaped
at them in astonishment, no words within reach.

"I know it's kind of trite. Flowers. Hope you don't mind. . . ."

"Mind?"

"Most of the girls up where I come from would have laughed me out of the house if I brought them flowers."

"Yankee girls don't like flowers?"

"I'm sure some do, but the ones I know think . . ."

Ginger could not stop herself. She stood up and lurched toward him to hug his neck. Their mouths met in a clumsy bump that almost hurt, and their kiss was brief and graceless. But she just had to do it. They laughed, parted, sat back down, looked at their food. Ginger still held the flowers. *I'm in love,* she told herself as she got back up and looked for a tall glass to put them in, since she didn't own a vase. She filled the glass with water, stuffed the flowers in, and set it on the table. When they looked at each other again they laughed. His eyes were a little watery, she thought. He was moved.

I'm in damn love.

*****

He picked up his fork and began to eat. "So, quit school, went to work. How do you like the real world?" he asked.

"I ain't never lived nowhere else."

Another eye lock, another smile. Ginger felt better and better. They both ate for a few moments. She put a dab of muscadine jelly on her biscuit. They were not her best ones, she saw, but they weren't bad. She watched him taste a bit of everything. The percolator bubbled and wheezed behind her. She watched him close his eyes until he'd swallowed what he had in his mouth, then open them as if he were surprised.

"This is quite good," he said.

Quite. The word made her laugh.

"I'm serious. It's delicious."

"I know." She could see she'd put him off course a bit. He didn't seem to take it bad, though. He ate a little more, his eyes open now. "That was very conceited," she added quickly. "What I really meant was I know you're serious."

"You couldn't hate reading too much; you read magazines. At least one book."

"The only book worth reading," she said.

"How long have you been out of school?"

"Two years and two months."

He sat back and looked surprised. "You're eighteen?"

"And two months."

He raised an eyebrow at her. She liked that. "How old are you?" she asked.

"Twenty-six." He grinned. "I thought you were twenty-one or two."

"Fooled you."

The longer they ate the more slowly they ate. She tried to give him more ham, more grits, more orange juice, but he said he was full. They drank some coffee. He liked his black; she liked milk and three spoonfuls of sugar in hers.

"So, where do you think we can find some hay? Right in the neighborhood, huh? I'll bet this little apartment complex used to be a pasture. . . ."

"We'll git some somewheres." She tried to do a common sense check, the way Reba told her she needed to learn how to do. Common sense wasn't what she was interested in right then, she knew. "I think we oughta just talk first."

He paused, his cup midway between his mouth and the table. "We haven't been talking already?"

"I mean, *really* talk." She saw hesitation in his eyes, but when she reached to touch his hand, his face relaxed into a cautious grin. She stood up, his hand still in hers. "C'mon."

*****

She led him to her bedroom. A quilt lay over the sheets, and she tossed it to the foot of the bed in a single flick of her wrist. She kicked off her sandals and lay down on her side facing him, her elbow on a pillow, cheek in her hand. She patted the space beside her. "What are you, scared of me?"

He still half-smiled, but he did seem nervous. "Do you always talk with strangers this way?"

"You strange all right, but you ain't all *that* strange." She waited for him to laugh, but they only continued to look at each other. She saw that his hands trembled as he bent to unlace his boots. She watched the top of his head for signs of thinness in his hair; and seeing none made her imagine their babies, dark-haired but a bit reddish in the right light, clear-eyed and peering at everything, always ready to smile. The babies multiplied before her eyes, stretching in a long line coming up the mountain, at the crown of which she sat to receive each child in the unqualified love of her open arms. Marcus stood back up, red-faced for a moment. He grinned—a little stupidly, she thought—which made him seem all the sweeter. When he ran his fingers through his hair, Ginger had to wait a moment to make sure her voice would sound normal. Then she patted the bed again.

"Talk to me."

Marcus slid onto the bed, not too close to her but not too far away, either. He assumed the same position as she did, cheek on his hand, elbow sunk into his pillow.

"You start," he said. "I'll try to keep up."

"I ain't that good of a talker."

"Brothers and sisters?"

"Fourteen. Six half-brothers, eight half sisters."

"So you're the youngest."

"The baby," she said. "But I can't stand none of them and they can't stand me."

"Jealous."

"Just ugly at me all the time. Saying ugly things."

"Like what?"

Ginger wasn't about to tell him. She'd backslid twice in her life, but somehow Earlene and Jasper had found out and told all the others—tricked her into admitting not just what she'd done but who she did it with.

"Just ugly." She reached to touch his hair, then withdrew immediately. "I been wanting to do that all day," she said.

He touched her in the same way but his hand stayed longer than hers had. She worked her way closer and kissed him, soft at first and then harder. But no tongue. He didn't try. She liked that. He knew how to kiss with just his lips. How to almost bite with them. Her arm crawled around his shoulder, his arm draped over her hip. The kiss paused as she pulled a few inches away, but the loose embrace stayed.

"I ain't done talking yet."

"Talk away. Great conversation so far."

"You gonna get the wrong impression about me."

"How could I possibly do that?"

"I'm just affectionate, that's all. You ain't married, right?"

"Never had the pleasure. Or was that pain?"

She watched closely for the nervous eyelid or stiffer arm muscle that she was used to seeing whenever she tested men by saying the word *married*.

"I'm not actively looking for a wife," Marcus said, "but I'm not actively *not* looking either." He paused. "In case you were wondering."

*****

Ginger knew she was willing to sin at that moment—beyond willing, *fixing* to—and that made her begin to hate herself. But she kept thinking also that maybe God wanted her to sin just then so that she'd get a lesson out of it. She was sure she'd got a lesson the two other times she backslid, and the second time she even got a blessing; she convinced a wayward man that he should go back to his wife, and when she saw them together at church the next Wednesday night, she got a blessing just from seeing *him* get one. She even got over being mad at him for not telling her he was married. God worked in mysterious ways, she'd sure figured that out.

Marcus moved his hand so that his wrist rested just above her hip in that little valley that was one of her favorite parts of herself. She couldn't keep her fingers out of the hair at the back of his neck.

"You're not talking," she said.

He studied her a moment, his eyes squeezing into that squint she liked.

"If we don't keep talking, we might get in trouble, laying here like this."

"I'm already in trouble," he said.

When she kissed him again, her leg slid over his and pulled his thigh almost against her. She was the one who started with the tongue, knowing as she did it that tasting a man's tongue was the weakest spot in her warm, moist soul. But it was all right this time because she could feel, more surely than she ever had, the bright abyss of true, lasting love that they were approaching. Together. Not just her. And besides, Jesus would forgive her eventually.

She rolled on top of him and sucked with small, long lip bites at his mouth and cheeks and eyes. She held his wrists against the pillow just above his head, rested her breasts against his, their lips brushing slowly back and forth, past and against each other; sometimes the tips of their tongues brushed, too and stopped a moment to plunge and run away again.

Ginger bad wanted to sin right then and there, but some voices tried to stop her while others egged her on. *Go ahead*, they said; *it's God's will*. She was confused, as she tended to get at times like these. She had to ask Marcus The Question, and she promised herself she would believe him when he said yes, whether it was true or not.

She pulled away, just far enough to see him clearly and know for sure. She said a quick prayer, asking the Lord not to make His ways too mysterious right now, and she kept her eyes hard on Marcus as the prayer went through her mind.

"Is Jesus Christ your Lord and Savior?" she asked.

She watched Marcus's eyes back away, and as they fled, so did she. She felt like a lump of weight on him, and the hard bone of her pelvis became a brick against his cement leg. His eyes were closed. She studied the blankness of his lids, glad she'd asked what she'd asked. For once. The warmth in her still lingered, but now it leaned against the ice box, not the stove. She crawled off him, embarrassed, angry but trying to convince herself that she felt relieved. She lay back, away from him.

He opened his eyes. "No," he said. "In all honesty, I can't say that's quite true."

"But He *is*."

Marcus shrugged, his eyes now a hostile silence, even when he spoke. "Maybe for you."

"Open your heart and He'll come in."

"Sorry. Not my trip."

"But you can do it if . . ."

"Look. I don't mean to sound . . . I dunno, ugly, as you call it. But where I come from, it's considered kind of impolite to ask a person about his religion. Especially at a time like this."

He sighed, but she heard no agony in his sigh. *Thank you, Lord,* she thought, her eyes closing. Her heart still slapped along too fast, and she tried to calm herself, listening to the morning through her closed eyes—a lawnmower, boys' voices shouting from so far away that she thought she was imagining them. She listened a moment to the whir of the other apartments' air-conditioners.

She felt him leave the bed in a single movement and stand there watching her. "Maybe we can talk about this some other time," he said. "Maybe we should go look for some hay right now. What do you think?"

She got up and went to the small desk in the corner of the bedroom. "Tell you what. How about if I was to draw you a little map of a couple places right down yonder that I think probably got some hay they'd give you?"

"I'd kind of hoped you'd come with me."

He sounded a bit sad, a bit boyish, but his boyishness no longer appealed to her. She doubted that they could ever talk about much, not unless he was willing to see things the way she knew he should. She scribbled, knowing she was writing too fast for him ever to be able to read it. But it was done now, and she wanted it to be over as quickly as possible so she could be embarrassed without an audience.

"Here." She avoided his eyes by pointing with the pen at what she had written. "You go here, and then turn here at the Shell station, and it's about two miles down this road, and this other place I think maybe's got some is . . ."

"Now I wish I'd lied."

She could see that his sorrow was as strong as hers, his mind just as made up as hers. "I woulda knowed right away."

He reached for the map, folded it and put it in his shirt pocket. "Well. Thanks for the breakfast."

Her eyes fled. "Sure."

"Can we maybe be friends?"

She felt a mild pump of tears, so she kept her eyes turned away. Part of her wanted to say yes, but another part of her thought she owed him at least as much honesty as he'd shown her. "I don't see how. Do you?"

He stood there, making no move to leave. How could she mess things up so badly every single time, she wondered. She told herself she should be polite and get up from the chair and see him to the door, but he was already going, and now he was only a sound on her steps, and then he was the sound of his truck and the breeze, and then he was no sound at all.

"Damn," she said. "Not you, Lord. Just in general."

She looked at the table of dirty dishes, started to pick them up, then put them back on the table. She'd do them later, she told herself. Right then she needed a nap. She wished it wasn't a holiday and that she had to go to work, where she wouldn't have time to think about things.

You Don't Understand, Garçon

for J.P. Donleavy

*T*wo vans full of policeman with riot helmets and shotguns
arrived and entered the building across the street from the bank,
where they went upstairs to the roof and stationed themselves
overlooking the small, curious crowd and the Brinks trucks in
the street below. The Farmers Trust was only a tiny platoon in
the nation's financial army, but it was the biggest bank in Vermont, and thoroughly worthy of extra security on moving day.

"The people who would try to stick up an operation like this
don't live in Vermont, they only live in the most dangerous cities
in the country," observed Stoke Montgomery, the senior executive vice president of the bank, the number two man.

"Yessir," Martin answered. He was the new janitor on the night
shift. During the day, Martin was a college student. Stoke Montgomery had taken a liking to him, pointing out that it was rare
these days to find a young person who worked full-time and also
went to school full-time. Although Martin knew several people
who both worked and went to school full-time, he always agreed
with Montgomery. "Yessir."

Montgomery patted his holstered pistol and smiled as he
scanned the cops on the roof across the street. Montgomery had a
reputation for being a terror in the presence of his immediate
underlings, the vice presidents and branch managers. But he was
always friendly to the rank and file, the tellers and secretaries and
computer keypunch people, especially if they were young. Montgomery was tall and thin and pitched forward, as if he'd never
quite recovered from a kick in the stomach. He was still brown-
haired, but his manner of speaking and moving seemed arduous
and old. He seldom smiled, and his face flushed with instant wrath
whenever something went wrong—or when he *thought* something
could go wrong. Today he was in the best mood Martin had seen
in the month that Martin had worked at the bank.

Montgomery nodded toward Archie and Goose, the two old
janitors, who stood in the street directing traffic around the Brinks
trucks. They, too, wore holstered pistols, although Montgomery
had not given either man bullets when he issued them guns for
the day.

Now Montgomery nudged Martin and nodded toward Archie

and Goose.

"I'm going to give those two about three hours to bury the hatchet, which they probably won't have the brains to do. And then I'm going to fire them."

Martin got the hint: he was to let Archie and Goose in on what he'd *overheard* Montgomery say. "Yessir."

"Or maybe I should just give them bullets for their guns," Montgomery added. "Things would probably take care of themselves, eh?"

At the old bank, Goose and Archie alternated weekly on the night shift, so Martin listened for one week to Archie complain about Goose, and the next week to Goose complain about Archie.

"I just do my job and go home," Archie always said. "The other one, he thinks he's in Hollywood. He don't do half the work I do." Archie moved only as much as he had to on his game leg, and just stood in one place with his hands on his hips most of the time. His hair was thin and gray, combed straight back, and his tight-lipped glare served notice that he was the only person around the bank who had a grain of sense.

Goose was the opposite. His round, toothless smile and jutting chin chattered constantly and, often, incomprehensibly. When he wasn't talking, his massive jaws gummed a wad of chewing tobacco. He was big and stooped, with pure white hair cut in a flat-top and a red face that got redder when he drank. He wore a wide rubber band to keep his black-framed glasses clasped to his skull. His arms were as big as fireplace logs. Goose loved to lean in the doorway of the bookkeeping department and tell stories to the nine women who worked the bookkeeping department's night shift. His eyes would wander from one to another as he tried to distract them—an unlikely possibility, since the women were allowed to go home as soon as they finished their work. But on winter nights, as the women waited for the buses to travel the snowy roads of Northern Vermont and bring in the checks and deposits from the branch banks, Goose and his stories were cautiously welcomed and not summarily ignored.

He'd been a carnival wrestler during The Depression, and when he wasn't working, he'd ridden the rails with the hobos. He'd worked picking cotton in the Deep South, and he'd been a deck hand on a Yugoslav freighter at the very time the Germans were trying to invade Yugoslavia. The ship was on its way to Australia, and her captain was so upset over the news of the invasion that he stopped the ship in the middle of the Pacific Ocean and drifted for eight days, trying to decide what to do. The crew was nearly out of food and water when they finally reached the Philippines, where they were taken prisoner by the Japanese and held for two months in a jungle prison camp before they were released and set back out to sea with a month's supply of food, but minus their cargo of wool. Martin had also heard Goose say the ship was carrying olive oil, but that was all right; Goose never told a story the same way twice.

Goose and Martin talked French when they worked together. Martin had learned to understand Goose's garbled dialect, and the two would sometimes have a beer together at The Black Cat Cafe on those nights when they got off work early enough. Martin mostly enjoyed working with Goose, except that the constant complaining about Archie got tiresome. When Martin asked Goose why he hated Archie, Goose said it was because Archie faked a disability to get sympathy and overtime. For the past year, Goose claimed, Archie had gotten all the overtime, whereas it used to be divided evenly. Goose needed at least a little overtime since his wife didn't have a job. Archie's wife did; she worked part-time as an egg sorter on a farm in Colchester.

"The gimp he get all of it an' me I don't get none. Dat ain't right. Sometime I tink I wear my arm in a sling. Maybe den I get some overtime."

"Talk to Mr. Montgomery. He's the working man's hero, they say."

"Talk to Montgomery? Dat like talk to the wall. He don't hear nothing nobody say. An' if he tink I'm gonna work as hard down at dat new place as I work up here all dem years, he ain't got a single brain between dem ears. You see him hire a special truck jus' to move Mr. President sword collection to the new building?"

They'd all laughed about that. The bank's president was a member of the Society for Creative Anachronism, a group that met regularly to dress in Medieval armor and costumes, joust on horseback, read Arthurian legends aloud to each other by candle light. The president kept an impressive sword collection on the wall in his office, and a few days before the bank's official moving date, two men in full armor arrived in the evening to move the swords to the new building. Stoke Montgomery had come in especially to oversee the operation.

"Dey a lot more interested in dem sword den you an' me," Goose had pronounced grimly, taking the fun out of a perfectly absurd moment.

It was funny, Martin had noticed, how Goose and Archie changed as you got to know them. Goose was fun at first, but the better you knew him the more he came across as a whiner.

Whereas Archie, who had spoken no more than ten words, counting grunts, during the two weeks he and Martin had worked together, now seemed the more amusing of the two.

"I fixed his ass one night," Archie told Martin. "I put red pepper in his chew. No tall tales *that* night."

"Hmmmm. I guess that explains why he's so fond of you."

"I don't care what he thinks. I do my work and go home."

Archie was also one of the most efficient workers Martin had ever observed, and he was grateful that it was Archie, not Goose, who trained him. After spending his first week with Archie, Martin felt exhausted just watching Goose swab and sweat, flood the sinks and toilets with disinfectant, vacuum all the floors every night, and rub down the mirrors with Windex until even the cracks were gone.

No swabbing the floors and sink counters for Archie. Look around first. If you see a spot that needs to be removed, spray it with the Windex you carry at all times, dry it with the towel you carry at all times. If the toilets smell, give them a shot of Pinesol. Keep plenty of toilet paper and paper towels on your cart.

"Make sure the place is clean," Archie reasoned, "but don't overdo it. It's only a bank. It ain't home."

*****

The Brinks trucks were loaded and about to depart. The people on the sidewalk began to clap, and Martin wondered why. Was it because the money seemed safe? A TV camera crew approached, and Martin watched Montgomery draw himself up to full height and prepare a smile.

"Mr. Montgomery, how has the move proceeded so far?"

Montgomery looked at his watch. "Not too bad. I'd say we're a little ahead of schedule—about forty-seven seconds to be exact."

Martin moved apart from Montgomery so as not to appear in the camera. Montgomery took two more questions and ended with a nod. When the trucks, reporters and audience were gone, he sauntered toward Martin, who waited by the door.

"So . . . I guess the hard part's done," Montgomery said, leading Martin inside. "I don't recall seeing you in a while. How's school?"

"Very good, Sir. I got an A on a chemistry exam. I've been celebrating."

Montgomery stuck out his lower lip approvingly and nodded. "Congratulations. And just how have you been celebrating?"

"I've been reading an excellent novel, Sir."

Montgomery snorted. "Don't college kids *drink* anymore?"

"Oh, yes Sir. I drink while I read."

Montgomery's smile returned. "Good. In fact, that's very mature. In a few years, you'll even be able to watch television at the same time as you're drinking and reading. Keep up the good work."

Montgomery was usually critical of people with long hair and sloppy blue jeans, but he overlooked Martin's appearance. Martin knew that Montgomery liked to watch him buff the floors while he listened to his cassette recordings of French verb conjugations.

"Keep an eye on things for me at the new bank. You understand?"

"Spying, Sir?"

"Don't inflate the request. You don't have to *report* anything. I'm just asking you to use your judgement. If you ever see anything getting out of hand, do something about it. And don't let me know unless it's absolutely necessary."

"Yes, Sir."

"I'm holding you directly responsible for anything that goes wrong during the reception down at the new bank tonight. If Goose is drunk, take him home. If he's sober, keep him out of public view. I'll be over later."

*****

With his hair hanging down into his eyes and a constant smirk on his thin, pockmarked face, Bud Mooreland could not avoid looking like the petty criminal he had always been. In his senior year of high school, he was caught stealing money from the principal's desk and was expelled from school. The judge who heard the case told Bud he could go to jail for sixty days, or go in the army for two years. Bud went in the Army and was stationed in Saigon as a mechanic, where he stole vehicle parts and sold them on the black market to the Viet Cong. During the two weeks before he left Saigon, he sold them an entire Jeep, component by component. It was his favorite war story to tell.

Bud smuggled about ten thousand dollars worth of marijuana into the United States when he came home. He lived off his sales for almost a year before he finally had to go to work. He had few skills, even after Army mechanic school, but a local soft drink distributor who was known to hire veterans gave Bud a job delivering to the downtown office building automats. Bud had been on the job for over two months and had pilfered only lightly. First of all, he couldn't figure out a way to beat the inventory system. Second, pilfering ten dollars worth of soft drink hardly seemed worth the high risk of getting caught.

What did interest Bud was that one of the banks he serviced was in the process of moving, and that struck Bud as an undefined but tantalizing opportunity. He studied the operation every moment he could. He had already made friends with one of the janitors, a quiet old guy who limped, and learned that the bank had no security guards.

Bud studied the layout of the old bank building and the new, where he helped install the drink machines. He knew no one would be able to get anything from the main vault, but he'd noted that the safe deposit boxes were not specifically protected in the old building. Bud knew that people kept all manner of things in safe deposit boxes, from precious gems and significant sums of money to photos of grandmothers in little lockettes. He learned from Archie that the contents of the safe deposit boxes would be moved separately from the contents of the main vault and at a different time. And that the move would not be as closely guarded as the moving of the main money.

A coherent scheme began to take life in Bud's mind. He figured that with a partner and a couple of security guard uniforms, he could cash in. He knew most of the small-time criminals in Burlington. There was Billy Weir. Everyone who knew him called him Billy Weird. Billy had been taunting Bud to figure out a way to knock off one of the places where he delivered Coke. Billy was in law school. It was not that he was trying to go straight; he'd simply decided to become a lawyer after the first time he was busted. Lawyers not only made money, he'd observed, they also knew their way around every obstacle in the modern world. So now Billy, who had cut his hair short when everyone else was growing it long, wore suits that he bought at the Good Will store, and had a barber trim his blond van dyke. His neatness, however, was no mask for his scoffing air and snide eyes.

Bud knew that to look like a security guard, he'd have to get a haircut, too. It would be worth it, he decided. He had tried to get to know everyone he could in the lower echelons of the bank. He'd given many of them free Cokes at one time or another—all the janitors, all the tellers. None of them would find it odd when he showed up moonlighting as a security guard.

Bud planned everything down to the tiniest detail, then he talked for hours to Billy Weird, telling him how it could be done. Billy Weird nodded as he pored over Bud's crude drawings of the new bank, noting the proximity of the safe deposit department to an unmonitored door leading outside. Bud told Billy that the evening security force, if you could call it that, consisted of just two old men and a college kid.

*****

When Martin arrived at the new bank, he found the lobby full of people. He could see that they were mostly hungry tellers and assistant branch managers who were trying to eat every smoked salmon croissant and Brie cracker laid out in the lush forests of parsley and kale that covered the long, linened tables. They also labored to suck the bar dry of Miller High Life and Cold Duck. A four-piece jazz band played to the unlistening crowd, and an announcer drew door prize winners' names out of a hat between the band's numbers. The hat was held by a smiling young lady in a black, sequined cabaret dancer's outfit, tuxedo jacket, spike heels.

The sky-lighted lobby was like an atrium, Martin noted, with enormous rubber plants, weeping figs, dracenas, calamondin orange and sweet-scented frangipani. There were hanging baskets of fuschia and impatiens, spider plants and Swedish ivy. He wondered why he had not yet heard Goose complain about all the new plants they would have to water.

The place was too noisy, Martin thought—not at all what a bank was supposed to be in the evening. He was dry-mouthed and antsy, thinking about his assignment concerning Goose, and wished that everyone who didn't belong there after six o'clock would go home so he could dim the lobby's harsh lights and finally enjoy the natural, soothing silence of an after-hours bank.

Martin spotted Montgomery, who beckoned him over, then stepped apart from the small cluster of people with whom he'd been conversing. His expression slipped from congenial to irate in a single blink.

"What in hell's going on upstairs?"

"Sir?"

"A group of people were making a little tour of the place. Wanted to see what goes on here at night. Said some little runt of a woman chased them off. Told them to mind their own goddamn business."

"Ah. Val. The night bookkeeping supervisor. . . ."

"These were officers of the bank. And directors. Just who the hell does she think she is?"

"Night supervisor of bookkeeping."

Montgomery snorted. "If I wasn't busy, I'd fire her. I'll do it in the morning. Where's Goose?"

"I don't know, Sir. . . ."

Montgomery's red face flushed to nearly brown. "You don't know? Your primary assignment for the night, and you don't *know*?" Montgomery abruptly turned away. "Get out of my sight."

Martin got out of the lobby as quickly as he could and went looking for Goose. Montgomery was right in wanting someone to keep tabs on Goose, but, Martin reminded himself, Montgomery had no way of knowing how difficult that could be. When

Goose didn't like something, he drank. The more he drank, the less he liked whatever had propelled him to drink in the first place. And Goose, by his own account, had plenty of reason to drink.

Martin had been to Goose's house once to watch a ball game. It was a small, stuffy apartment above a bar over on North Street. Small flaps of wallpaper that had peeled away quivered in the breeze from the five fans that were all trained on Goose where he sat, fat and immobile in his ragged easy chair. He wore an old, stained undershirt, the kind with shoulder straps, and a Montreal Expos hat that looked as if it had been sat on as much as worn. Goose didn't try to get up when Martin came inside, but his toothless oval smile was as big as a grapefruit.

"*Garçon! Entrez!*"

Yvonne, Goose's wife, was as wide as she was tall in her green bathrobe, and her straight, matted hair was cut in a way that made Martin think she had put a bowl over her head and cut it herself. Her smile seemed a bit clownish, self-conscious at having a visitor, but somehow hospitable as well.

"*Va chercher le garçon une bière,*" Goose ordered. "A cold one. And get one for me."

"You don't need no more beer," Yvonne said. Looking back at Martin she shook her head. "My, my . . . ain't he awful?"

"Goddamn it, don't tell me what I need and don't need."

"Get your own beer," a third person in the room said quietly. Martin noticed a woman he guessed to be thirty-five or forty. She wore a middle-aged blue print dress, black flats with white ankle socks, and far too much lipstick. Her short brown hair was so tightly curled that Martin imagined it must have given her a headache.

"This is Yvette, my daughter," Goose said, giving her an unfriendly glance. "She don't like the Expos; she likes dem Red Sox of Boston." He said it with such contempt that Martin's eyes cut back to him for an instant.

"Hello," Yvette said, her eyes trained on the TV.

"I said get him a *beer!*"

Yvonne jumped at the sternness in Goose's voice, but her smile never wavered. "Ain't he awful?" she repeated.

It was like that for the two hours Martin stayed there; Goose bellowed for more beer, Yvonne objected but obeyed, and Yvette either watched TV or scornfully eyed Goose and from time to time shook her head at Martin. When the Red Sox scored and the noise from the bar downstairs grew louder, Goose twice struggled out of his chair, leaned out the open window, stomped his big, angry foot and yelled, "*Shuddup! Maudits bâtards!*"

After his outbursts, Goose would calm down a little and turn his toothless smile toward Martin, as if he were expecting some gesture of approval. He seemed more happily drunk than angrily drunk, and Martin was relieved with the change.

"He act like that at work?" Yvette asked. She sat with her legs crossed, leaning forward a bit. Martin thought she seemed very pleasant in a detached way. He especially liked the way she stood up to Goose, whom Martin began to perceive as just a big, powerless peon who took out his frustrations on his family. A harmless bear, not the psychotic gorilla that some, like Stoke Montgomery, or Archie, or Valette Beaupre, the night bookkeeping supervisor, considered him.

"Some nights," Martin answered.

"He's okay when he works days," she said. "But when he works nights, he starts drinking in the afternoon. I'm surprised they haven't fired him."

Goose's good humor evaporated. "Dey fire me and I kill one of dem no good bastards." He turned his anger on Yvette. "Don't go talking about me or I talk about you. An' you know what I mean."

Yvette and Yvonne suddenly seemed uneasy. They began to jabber in a French so mangled that Martin understood hardly any of it. Goose's eyes narrowed and became angry again. He leaned forward in his chair.

"You know something, Garçon? She ain't normal. She twenty-six years old and never had a date. Never been laid. I been ten years waiting for a grandchild, and she refuse every offer for a date. And she don't get many."

Yvette rose from her seat and retreated to a back room, closing the door quietly behind her. Her mother followed.

"My, my . . . ain't that awful?" Yvonne said as she left, the pained smile still frozen on her.

Martin left a few minutes later. By that time, Goose seemed remorseful as he begged Martin to stay and have another beer. But Goose made no move to apologize to Yvette, so Martin left.

For the next few days, Martin avoided Goose at work, but when Goose finally apologized for his behavior that afternoon, Martin could not help but forgive him. Martin acknowledged that he liked Goose and felt sorry for him. Goose was one of those two-sided people from whom you had to take the bad with the good, if you wanted to be friends.

*****

Martin looked for Goose in the mailroom and the employee lounge, then went upstairs to the bookkeeping department to see if any of the night shift women had seen him. Val said she hadn't, and that she also hadn't particularly missed him. Valette and Goose usually spoke French together, when they talked at all. Val, as she put it, had no use for a drinker.

"You keep him the hell out of here when he's drinking," she told Martin his first night on the job. Val was small, short-haired, quick in her movements, and always serious. Everything she said, from hello to goodnight, sounded like a threat.

"Take these trays into the computer room or I'll give you a haircut," she often told Martin. The bookkeeping girls loved to tell about the time little Val picked Goose up one night when he was drunk, carried him out of the bookkeeping department, then locked the door to keep him out.

Martin went back to the mail room to check the time cards. Goose had clocked in at four-thirty, so he had to be somewhere in the building. Martin recalled Montgomery's certainty that Goose would be drunk. The chances were about ninety-nine percent, Martin agreed, recalling Goose's reasons for resisting the move.

"Dey ain't gonna have no windows you can open over dere. It ain't gonna be safe if dere's a fire."

"Use the door if there's a fire."

"And dem elevators ain't safe, Garçon."

"Why not?"

"Dey go up too high. Dey go five floors."

"Some elevators go up a hundred floors."

"Dat's what I mean. Dey ain't safe. An' another ting, all dem doors an' dey ain't got no security to cover dem."

"No, they have locks."

Goose always shook his head. "Garçon, you don' unnerstan'. It ain't gonna be like it was here. The customers like to come here. Dey ain't gonna go no extra five blocks to the bank. Dis one's a nice little bank. Dat ting down by the lake is ugly."

"You think people pick a bank by the way it looks?"

"Dey pick what dey used to. Dey ain't used to go all the way down dere. Dat place is too big. And dey ain't no security."

"There's no security here, Goose."

"We don't need none here. Dis place don't look big enough to rob. Dat one does. I don't like it one damn bit."

Goose was ready to attack anything that night, four days before the move. He noticed Martin's cassette recorder and lashed out at that. "You don't learn no good French that way, Garçon," he said. "Not the way us Canadians talk."

"I like the voices of the women on the tapes. Two of them. I have dreams about them sometimes."

But Goose had no use for the French that night. The women were all sluts, the men were all chickenshit, and the streets were filthy and smelled bad from people pissing in the gutters.

"I was dere when we liberate Paris. Fifty-second Airborne. Dem French dey run around yellin', '*Nous avons gagné la guerre!*' 'Bullshit,' I says to dem. '*C'est les Américains ont gagné la guerre.*'"

"I thought you were on a Yugoslav freighter in the South Pacific Ocean during la guerre?"

"Dat was at de beginning. I was in France at de end of la guerre."

But where is he now, Martin wondered as he searched from office to office, floor to floor. In one office he found a dismal bit of evidence: an empty pint-sized whiskey bottle—the brown bag wrapped tightly around it in Goose's trademark way—alone in an otherwise brand-new, unblemished waste basket.

*****

Bud walked into the basement delivery lobby of the bank as if he owned it. Billy Weird followed. From her glassed-in office, Floss, the switchboard operator, controlled the entrance, and when she saw the Coca-Cola man dressed in a security guard's uniform, she let him in without hesitation. The door knob made a long, beckoning buzz.

"Hi, Bud. Change jobs?" Floss was a small, white-haired woman to whom Bud had given many Cokes. Her curly hair and wire-rim glasses made him think of every school teacher he'd ever detested.

"Working part-time as a guard. Billy, this here's Floss. She lets folks in and out, as you might have observed just now."

Billy bowed and smiled stiffly. "Pleasure to meet you."

"Nice to meet you. There's food up in the lobby." She nudged her plate of hor d'oeuvres toward them. "Shrimp, Swedish meatballs, chicken fingers. You name it." She seemed very satisfied, as if she were the one who had bought and prepared the food.

As the men walked toward the employee lounge, Billy Weird said, "I didn't know you had so much personality."

Bud smiled. "I know who to give a Coke to. I know most of these people by name. And that's how they know me."

Billy Weird was enjoying the moment. His favorite position in life was that of observer. He loved to watch people who weren't watching him, and he saw that Bud was busy watching himself. That gave Billy a comfortable sense of separation from Bud. As far as Billy was concerned, they were in this together only if it worked. If something went wrong, it was Bud's gig. Billy would deny any knowledge of what Bud had planned.

They passed more people Bud knew, and he shook their hands and wished them great success in the new location. Bud surprised even himself with his friendliness and realized that he would have to be careful; he could blow his cover by trying to impress Billy Weird. By the time they ran into the college kid, Martin, Bud had made himself wary of everyone.

"New clothes and a new nose," Martin said as he walked off the elevator and nearly stepped on Bud's foot. "Or did you just shave?"

Bud mustered a smile. "All three, I guess."

"Are you working for the bank now?" Martin asked.

"No. IBM sent us to keep and eye on the computer while it gets moved. In case somebody tries to steal it."

Martin jerked his head a bit. "Oh. I thought they moved the computer this morning?"

"They did. We're just supposed to be here with it for twenty-four hours."

"Well, good luck. Don't let it think too much."

As soon as Martin was out of sight, Bud and Billy Weird went back to the office next to the fire exit, where Bud had learned from Archie that the contents of the safe deposit boxes would probably arrive, since that was where the safe deposit clerk's office would be. Bud knew which office Archie meant and knew that he and Billy Weird could wait there. They slipped inside, closed the door, and turned on a desk lamp in the small, windowless room.   Bud took handcuffs and cloth gags out of the attaché case he carried. Billy Weird checked his gun, then he sat and watched Bud.

"What?"

"You," Billy said, smiling. "I never seen anybody who was so uptight think he was so cool."

*****

When he didn't find Goose on the upper floors, Martin went downstairs to the employee lounge to check there. He wondered how long it would take the bank's junior executives to finish the food and booze and go home. He pictured Val running them out of the bookkeeping department and savored the outraged look on Mr. Montgomery's face when he heard about it.

No Goose on the first floor. Martin made a quick tour of the bathrooms, which hardly looked used. He squirted one small spot on the mirror in the ladies' room and wiped it clean, then picked up some scraps of toiler paper from the floor. He would collect the trash later, he decided. After he found Goose.

Instead, it was Goose who found him. Martin had just put a

new roll of toilet paper in the corner stall when he heard the door crash against the wall. Goose stood in the doorway with a surprised smile as he looked at the small, black mark the door handle had made in the new sheet rock.

"Damn door open too easy," he said, turning his bleary, smiling eyes toward Martin.

"You okay?" Martin asked.

"I coont be better, me."

"Where's your gun?"

"I leff dat ting up at the old building. I don't like guns." He smiled his vast abyss of a smile and grabbed Martin by the arm. "Garçon, Garçon. Dey so many ting you don't unnerstan. . . ."

"You want to lie down and take a nap? Or go home?"

"Maybe dat nap is a good idea, Garçon. Ain't nuttin to clean."

"Where? In case I need you. . . ."

"Mail room." He stumbled back out the door, and the sound of his feet disappeared into the carpet in the corridor. Martin sighed, took a last look around the bathroom, checked the paper towel dispenser, and started out the door as Val pushed by him on her way in.

"Heard you terrorized some of the bank's icons of authority."

"They wanna come watch, make an appointment," she said. "You leaving or do I have to piss in front of you?"

Martin hurried out.

Now that he'd located Goose, Martin took the elevator to the fifth floor. He'd not had time yet to tour the new building, and now he glanced in each dark office, checking for trash in the wastebaskets. Every room was immaculate, every desktop paperless.

The last office in the executive suite was President Vick's. Martin could not resist sitting at the president's desk to look out through the wall-sized window at the sparse, flickering lights of the nighttime waterfront. The office faced Lake Champlain, and Martin imagined the sunsets the president would enjoy as the orange sky sucked itself down behind the Adirondack mountains across the lake each night. A gorgeous office, Martin thought, contrasting the sumptuous space with the cramped quarters of President Vick's office in the old building.

Martin glanced at the wall behind him to see if the president had arranged his swords the same way as in the old bank—the smaller estocs and rapiers surrounding the centerpiece, which was a magnificent two-hand, six-foot-long German sword from the fifteenth century. The smaller, more ornate swords were there, but the German was not. Martin jumped up from his seat. Goose had said he was going to take a nap, but Martin had not followed him to the mail room to make sure that was where he went.

Martin took the stairs back down to the lobby to make sure Goose had not decided to make an appearance there first. The reception guests were gone and the lobby was already in darkness, even though the mess from the party had not been cleaned up yet. He wondered why the safety lights were not on, then he realized that Goose might have shut them off.

As Martin watched, the lobby lights did come on, and Archie hobbled along the teller cages mumbling about the lights being off. Then Martin noticed Goose hiding behind a big rubber plant, with the sword from President Vick's office raised over his head.

When Archie hobbled by the small forest, the sword made a mighty swipe, humming through the air as it leveled three large rubber plants. Archie yelped and froze as goose raised the sword to swing again. *Thunk!* Branches of dracena and frangipani flew across the lobby floor. Now Archie fled as Goose lumbered through the mess, the sword singing through the empty air just above the stubs of once lush plants as Goose swung again and again and lurched toward Archie.

Archie screamed as he ran, but he found himself cornered in front of the office next to the fire exit.

"I see you run just den," Goose bellowed. "Bad leg, huh? I knew you was faking it all deze years!"

Archie pulled out his gun and pointed it unsteadily at Goose. "Stay away from me!"

Martin remembered that neither of them could see very well, so he snuck around back of the teller cages to the main light switch boxes and pulled every lever. The bank fell again to darkness, and Martin thought he could hear every piece of machinery in the building catch its breath in a sudden halt.

"Who's dat?" Goose demanded.

Martin heard a door slam and figured Archie had ducked into the office by the fire exit door. Goose pounded and kicked and swore in French. Martin heard a wooden crash and another hoarse scream from Archie and realized that Goose had broken down the door.

Then Martin heard hurried footsteps and glanced up to see Stoke Montgomery come barreling into the lobby, his gun drawn, his face pale and aged, the veins in his neck bulging like vines climbing a tree trunk.

Martin motioned to him to say nothing. Montgomery ducked down and scampered to where Martin was crouched behind the teller cages.

"What in hell is going on *now?*" Montgomery whispered

loudly.

"Goose and Archie."

"Oh. Something new. I thought you were in charge of this."

"Sir . . . I believe Goose dislikes change—and I know for a fact that he'd also like some grandchildren."

Montgomery's face blanched even more. "Remind me to retract whatever decent things I said about you this afternoon."

"Yessir."

*****

Billy Weird was trying to listen to the commotion in the lobby when the old janitor with the limp burst into the office where he and Bud were hiding. Archie slammed the door and tried to brace it shut. Something told Billy to ask no questions, just help the old guy keep the door shut. Bud caught on, too. All three tried to hold the door, but Goose blew in like a strong wind in a pond of reeds. Billy and Archie went flying against the wall, but Bud was knocked over the desk and onto the floor.

At that moment, the van carrying the contents of the safe deposit vaults pulled up outside the door. One of the drivers pressed the buzzer.

Goose bellowed at Billy Weir. "Who the hell are you?"

Billy tried to bolt past Goose, but Goose collared him, gave him a whack on the side of his head, threw him against the wall and held him there. With his free hand he grabbed Bud and dragged both of them out of the office. He pushed the door open with his rump while the guards who were carrying cardboard cartons that contained the safe deposit materials looked on in shock.

"Here," Goose said. "I tink dese two was up to someting."

One of the Brinks guards set his carton down and put handcuffs on Bud and Billy, then led them outside. The other guards kept carrying in their boxes, watching Goose and the gun and sword with apprehension.

Goose went back into the office where Archie sat on the floor, massaging his ankle. "You busted my leg, you friggin' ape!"

Montgomery stood up. "C'mon. . . ."

Martin heard a sound from the other direction and pulled Montgomery back down. "Wait," he whispered.

Val entered the lobby and looked contemptuously at the branches of the rubber plants that Goose had whacked off with the sword. She muttered in French, planting her hands on her hips and kicked the branches out of her way.

"Archie! Goose! Where are you two?"

The mumbling in the office where Archie was cornered stopped. Goose's voice was meek as he stuck his head out.

"What?"

"You get yourself out here and clean up this lobby. This is a brand new building and you two made a mess already." Her footsteps were fast and angry as she barged past Goose into the office.

"He started it," Archie moaned.

She glared at Goose. "And when you finish down here, you get yourself upstairs and clean that ladies' room!"

Goose came out, shoulders slumped, and trudged toward the rubber plants. Archie followed, dragging his game leg toward the elevator. The Brinks guards watched a moment, glancing at each other and smirking each time they carried in another carton. In the distance, a police siren quavered toward them, growing louder.

"All of it," she hollered at Goose, who had picked up only the largest branches.

Montgomery met the police outside while Martin watched through the glass door. The cops took Billy Weird and Bud from the Brinks guard, shoved them into a cruiser, and drove out of the parking lot.

Back inside, Montgomery mopped his forehead with a handkerchief as he slumped toward the stairwell. He motioned for Martin to follow him. They climbed three flights of stairs to Montgomery's office, where he collapsed into the chair behind his desk. After rubbing his eyes for a moment, he opened a drawer and took out a bottle of Scotch and two plastic glasses. He poured the glasses half full, then looked gravely at Martin.

"I'm putting you in charge of this project," he said.

"What project, Sir?"

"Get that door Goose broke down replaced, get new rubber plants to replace the damaged ones, and we'll just make believe none of this happened. Don't let me hear about any of it."

"No Sir."

"What about that woman? Does she have a big mouth?"

"Val. Pretty big. Yes, Sir."

"Ah, the infamous Val. Well . . . she's just here at night. Once we take care of the door and get the plants replaced, nobody'll believe her anyway." Montgomery nodded as he thought. "We'll set things up so that Archie goes home at four and Goose doesn't show up until four-thirty. Maybe they'll forget each other."

"Maybe, Sir."

"And in a couple of weeks I'll promote Val. She does a hell of a job."

"Yessir." Martin took his first sip of the whiskey. "Excellent job, Sir."

Montgomery continued to watch Martin. "I want you to understand that I'm *not* glossing this thing over. The fact is that Goose caught two would-be robbers. That's why I'm forgiving him for hacking the rubber plants to bits and generally scaring the shit out of everyone."

"I understand completely, Sir."

"Good." A faint smile broke. "Next to reading, drinking, and watching TV all at once, the surest sign of maturity is wisdom."

Martin nodded. "I always thought so myself, Sir."

Rest Areas

for Truman Capote

When I went to pick Opal up from dialysis, I was surprised to find her waiting outside, gaunt as ever but a little fleshier somehow than she looked the first time I'd seen her, a month earlier. Her eyes peered out from their cavernous sockets, and her cheek bones looked sharp enough to cut the hand that might touch them. But she smiled when I pulled up, and for the first time, I saw in that skeletal face and figure and thin, brown hair the remnants of what used to be a good looking woman—and before that a girl who had maybe been eager about a few things in life.

I was going to open the door for her, but she was inside before I could even put the car in park.

"Hello, Ben. Cully told me you'd be picking me up."

"He's got some big meeting this morning."

"Well . . . I hope he makes a bunch of money. Take that gal friend of his out to some fancy place." Opal took a deep breath, a sound that seemed almost exuberant, and looked straight ahead as we pulled away. "Th'ain't nothing like having your blood sucked out of you and cleaned up and put back in to make you feel like a rug that's been vacuumed real good."

I was ready for a barrage of pent-up chattiness, since I knew Cully was spending his nights at Colleen's and that Opal was usually alone. But she didn't unload any of it on me, or act like she resented Cully's staying away. I liked the way she looked around at the buildings and cars as we drove, and her delight with a fountain that erupted suddenly as we passed by. When she took a deep breath now and again, it seemed more like she was sucking in the fresh fall air than just gasping.

"Ain't them sages pretty," she pointed. "I used to grow red sages in my garden."

"Cully told me you liked to garden."

"Used to."

When we got to Cully's I offered to help her inside, but she said she could make it herself, and that she just needed to lie down and rest after the busy morning. She'd told me that dialysis meant sleeping or watching TV for three hours while the machine fixed her blood. I figured if Opal considered that a busy morning, she was closer to death than anyone I'd ever known.

*****

Opal did not glow the first time I met her. She sat like a faint, noontime shadow in the middle of her sagging couch, hunched over, struggling to sit straight but unable to lift her head to look directly at anyone or anything. Every unclothed bone jutted out. She made me think of a doctor's office skeleton, but one covered with this thin, splotched skin. Cully had told me she had some disease that ate away the bone, but he couldn't remember the name of it. And the rotting bones were really the least of Opal's problems. She had a bad heart, kidneys that no longer worked, and a mind, according to Cully, that recalled only the things he had done over the years that had made her angry.

"Like what?" I asked him as we drove down I-65 toward Mobile to bring her back to Birmingham to live with Cully.

"Nothing major. The usual adolescent stuff. Getting drunk. Getting in a few fights at school."

I had an idea he wasn't telling me everything.

Opal had this old Buick, a huge white land barge with lots of rust and bird shit all over it, and she refused to leave Mobile unless the car came, too. That's why I was along; I was going to drive the Buick. Cully and I carried Opal out to his Volvo—I mean literally carried her on a seat we made with our clasped arms. She came to life a bit when we picked her up, and she rested her skeleton arms across our shoulders. She weighed about as much as a balloon. She looked at me for the first time.

"I love that car," she said. "Don't wreck it."

Cully glanced at me over the top of her head and winked grimly. I got the impression that learning to keep his mouth shut when she said certain things had always been a test for him. She held onto my hand as we lowered her through the door and she adjusted herself on the seat. It was weird, holding those bones in my fingers that long, especially when she gripped hard to shift herself over another inch.

Cully walked with me back to the Buick. The car hadn't been started in two years, and it blew up a solid black cloud when I cranked it.

"This thing going to make it two hundred and sixty-five miles?" I asked him.

"Don't think of it as two hundred and sixty-five miles. Think of it as five hours. This car's only gotta run for five more hours out of its whole miserable life." The smoke rolled up around him. Hunched over, he coughed all the way back to his Volvo.

The Buick kind of wheezed when I put it in drive. I was pretty damned nervous driving on those bald tires. There was a lot of play in the steering wheel, and the brakes were real soft. We stopped to gas up and put in a quart of oil before we got on the Interstate. Fifty-five max, we agreed. The Buick ran just fine up into Escambia County, but then the temp light on the dashboard came on bright red and I had to pull over and just watch as the steam whistled out through the grille. Cully had gradually pulled ahead of me and didn't know I'd had to stop. I let the steam blow for awhile before I opened the trunk and found a thick rag to open the radiator with. There was an old plastic antifreeze jug back there, so I was able to fill the Buick up with water from the gully that ran alongside the highway. The Buick kept boiling over. I stopped at various exits to drink coffee and eat fried apple pies until the Buick cooled down enough for me to put in more water. It seemed as if the car was in open rebellion against being relocated.

The fourth time I stopped, I noticed that the water was coming out in a pretty good stream near the bottom of the block. The engine had blown a freeze plug. I looked around the parking lot near a hedge and found a twig of about the right size and carved it a bit with my pocket knife until it fit good and snug in the hole in the engine. After that the car ran like a champ. Not only did I make it to Birmingham, the Buick ran better the closer we got. When Cully came out to get the key from me and apologize for our getting separated, he looked pretty grim.

"Maybe she'll shut up now that the car's here," he said.

*****

I didn't see Cully for a couple of weeks after Opal moved in with him. I called him once or twice and got no answer, so I figured he was taking her out here and there. It turned out that I'd been calling when he was either bringing her to the doctor or to the emergency room, where they'd brought her back from the pretty much dead. Depending on the doctor or the medical student they saw, Cully got several versions of when Opal's passing might happen. Two weeks to two years, they said. Maybe shorter, maybe longer. When I did finally get over to Cully's and he told me all this, I could see that both of them probably hoped it would be closer to two weeks than two years. The tension between them was like two frayed ends of a downed power line that the wind blew together every few minutes.

Opal sat in the dark in the kitchen, her shadow hunched over the table as she slowly and incessantly stirred a cup of tea. "Eatin's about the only pleasure I got left in life, Cully," she said in a wheezing growl. "And all of a sudden you're *concerned* about me? Just 'cause I have a little fun when I eat?"

"I don't like having to clean up after you get sick."

"Hah! The truth is out. I figured it was something more like that than you giving a damn about me."

"That, too."

"The hell, you say."

Opal's kidney failure and trips to the dialysis center twice a week were causing Cully a real problem, he told me when he went out on the porch to smoke. Medicare was willing to pay for an ambulance to come pick her up and bring her back home from the treatments, but she insisted that a decent son would consider it his duty to drive her himself. A really decent son wouldn't have it any other way.

"I'm in the middle of a goddamn meeting and Mom has Angie come in to tell me come pick her up."

Cully had a high-powered day job at the time. Ten years earlier, when we met, we were working together as carpenters. Now Cully worked in a bank as a commercial real estate loan officer, and I was working nights, running the computer at a different bank. When you work at night you don't need as much sleep as people who work days.

"What time's her treatment?" I asked. "You drop her off on your way to work and I'll pick her up."

Cully got his old smile back, the one he always used to have when we were out hunting together, or shooting hoops. "I'm re-naming you," he said. "From now on you're *Saint* Ben. As in, *been* the savior of my damn life."

Poor old Cully wasn't used to having to take care of himself, let alone somebody else. Deferred adulthood, we used to call it. Five or six more beers, a twelve-point buck in the back of the pickup on a fall afternoon, and we might be able to defer it for the rest of the weekend, and from there it was a short hop to forever. But now we were both bearing down hard on thirty-five, and neither one of us had ever made provisions for the end of the camping trip.

*****

The next time I picked Opal up, she seemed more chipper and wanted to get some fried chicken and biscuits. I knew she wasn't supposed to eat that stuff, so I tried to talk her out of it.

"How about if I bought some for you, too," she said, setting her hand on my bare arm. She was much warmer than the handful of cold, dry bones that I'd met in Mobile in August, when everything but Opal was dripping wet.

"What do you, think you can bribe me or something?" I asked.

"I ain't above it."

So we did the drive-through window at KFC. She insisted on

KFC since she liked The Colonel's biscuits best. Fried chicken was fried chicken; it was the biscuits that counted, according to Opal. She tried to buy me some, too, but I don't much care for fried chicken. I got some tea, just to let her get me something for picking her up.

"You have to come in this time, whether you're going to eat or not," she said when we pulled up at Cully's.

"I do?"

"Yeah, I need somebody to get rid of the evidence after I finish." She broke a small, sunken smile.

✳✳✳✳✳

Cully's laugh sounded good on the phone. "Man, I don't know what you and Mom are doing—and I don't *want* to know—but she sure is in a good mood on dialysis days."

"She's pleasant company. Kind of entertaining, in a way."

"I'm glad she is for somebody. She sure gives *me* hell."

"How's her diet?"

"Man . . . Last night I came home from the gym early, and she's sitting there with a damned *pizza*. I had to phone all the pizza places in town and tell them not to deliver here. Mom threw a fit. Said I treat her like a child. I told her that's what happens when somebody *acts* like a child."

I felt guilty about taking Opal by KFC, but the fact was she never ate more than two bites of chicken and less than half of one biscuit. I always ended up finishing her food. I figured out after that first stop that it wasn't the food she wanted as much as it was the freedom to buy it if she chose to. I already knew about the pizza she was sneaking before Cully told me. Opal bragged to me every time I picked her up about all the ways she'd found to antagonize Cully. Her favorite one was something she hadn't even thought up herself, one of the nurses at the dialysis center had come up with it.

"I make him write down in a little bitty notebook how much I piddle and deftacate," she said. "Hell, it's the only way I can get his attention. He just comes home long enough to get a change of clothes for the next day, and then he's off to Colleen's. A son ought to pay a little more respect to his mother, don't you think, Ben? Is your mama alive?"

"No."

"Well, then. Tell Cully he better appreciate me while I'm still around. No, on second thought, don't; let him feel as guilty as sin when I'm gone."

We drove without talking for awhile, but before I took her to KFC, I told her we could make those stops only if she quit aggravating Cully. Back at Cully's, we sat on the couch and ate. While I lectured her, she set her hand on my thigh, near my knee, and looked at me with this mock sincerity.

"I'll take it easy on him. For you."

"Thanks." I stood up to go. Opal stood up, too. She looked a little unsteady on those twigs she had for legs.

"You know what Opal could really use?" she said with a coyness I hadn't seen in her before.

"What could Opal really use?"

"Cully never gives me a hug." She conjured up this girlish smile, and at that moment she just looked real cute.

"So . . . you want a hug."

"Do you mind?"

"Of course not."

She slipped into my arms like the wisp of a creature that she was. She was about exactly my height, so we fit together pretty nicely. Usually when people who don't have something going on hug, they pat each other on the back while they're hugging. The friendly hug as opposed to some other kind. Opal didn't pat my back, so I didn't pat hers. It was not a tight hug but it was a complete one, full frontal contact from the knees to the cheeks. It lasted maybe ten seconds, I don't know. It wasn't quick, though. And it wasn't passionate; nobody started breathing heavy or anything like that. It was just a hug. A good, warm one.

So that routine got added to dialysis days, along with the stops at KFC. Then a third routine came about. One morning Cully had to go to work early, before the dialysis center was open, and he wanted to know if I could bring Opal to the center *and* pick her up. When I went to get her, Opal was ready and waiting for me—in the old, white Buick.

"Ben, can we go in my car one time?"

I checked the twig I'd stuck in the freeze plug hole in the engine block. It was still there, still tight. When I lowered the hood, there was Opal with this worried curiosity and anticipation watching me through the front windshield. When I nodded that the engine looked okay, her smile exploded, she clapped her hands together and was just about dancing when I got in the car. Cully had warned me that Opal always felt sick and was pretty bitchy before she got her treatment, but that wasn't the case today.

"Me and this car got some memories," she said, glancing all around, especially toward the back seat.

After I dropped her off at the dialysis center, I drove the Buick to a car wash. They went through it from one end to the other, inside and out, three people altogether, since there weren't any other cars. They managed to get rid of the musty smell, so I had them put on new seat covers, the soft, fake fur kind.

Opal was really pleased. She sat in the middle of the seat, right next to me, her hand near my knee. At one point she rested her head on my shoulder.

"Where were you when I was seventeen?" she asked.

"I was probably a sperm on the big swim."

She squeezed my leg. "I always did like the young ones."

After that, Opal waited for me in the Buick on dialysis days, and she always sat close to me, and her eyes roamed all over the car as if every arm rest and radio knob summoned a specific memory. I got into the habit of driving by Cully's on my way to work at night so I could see that quiet glow of the bumpers and grill under the streetlights. I'd always glance up at Opal's lightless window. She went to bed early, she told me. It was a childhood habit she'd never tried to lose.

The way she looked at me when we were in the Buick together—this kind of electrical charge that sometimes just glowed and other times crackled—made me wonder not so much what Opal was thinking but what I was thinking. My best friend's mother?

"I love to see her happy," he had told me more than once. "I just never have known how to make it happen."

He was calling me two or three times a week to thank me for taking over both ends of the dialysis trips. "Man, I'm fixin' to get someone to carve a bust of your head so Mom can burn candles in front of it."

"You two getting along any better?"

"Yeah. We finally have something to talk about. You."

"Tell her I'm not all that interesting."

"Like hell. If I even told her you're actually a human being I'd be taking my life in my hands." He paused. "Look, man, I'm hesitant to even mention this, since you already spend half the week with Mom, but I need to ask one more favor. I've got a trade show in Dallas this weekend. Do you mind staying over here with her for a couple of days?"

"Can't she just call me if she needs anything?"

"She gets lonely. And she's too proud to actually ask for something. You can sleep in that brand new bed of mine. I'll even change the sheets for you."

So, when I got off work at six on Saturday morning, I drove to Cully's and let myself in with the key he'd given me. I tried to be real quiet so I wouldn't wake Opal, but Opal was not only up, she had breakfast waiting: orange juice, link sausages, pancakes, eggs, the works.

I hardly ever get hungry before noon, since I snack all night at work, but I sat down and dug in. The pancakes were so light my fork fell through the stack, which oozed with thick syrup and real butter. A dry, sweet, floury steam trickled up from the plate. The sun filled the window by the table and spread out inside the room. Opal sat at the table in what looked like a new, print house-coat, smiling at the cup of coffee between her hands.

"Heard from Cully?" I asked.

She shrugged. "Why would I hear from Cully?"

"No reason, I guess." I didn't really want to talk about Cully unless it was going to be something good, and I didn't want to think about anything but these pancakes. And this juice; one sip and I knew it was fresh-squeezed, with ice in it, as if she'd known all her life that was the way I liked it.

Her eyes followed my fork wherever it went. "You got any plans this weekend?" she asked.

"Yeah. I'm doing them. Right this second."

"I think we should do something exciting."

"Like what?"

"You ever been down at the coast this time of year? The brats are back in school. Ain't hardly nobody on the beach."

"Aha. You want to go down to Mobile for a visit."

"Visit? I want to go *home*. I don't belong here."

"But you sold your place."

She suddenly got the pale, cavernous look back, and her eyes narrowed. "Oh, no . . . did Cully sell my house on me?"

I felt a chill, even in the sunlight. It was a second or two before I could speak. "Opal, *you* sold that house. Don't you remember? That's why you had to move up here."

"The hell you say." She slapped the tabletop. "I'd never sell my house. If it's sold, Cully sold it. Why didn't you tell me?"

She had turned yellowish-white, the way she looked the first time I saw her, but now her eyes were cloudy instead of blank.

"And here I thought I still had my own place."

The sun glinted off the metal tops of the salt and pepper shak-ers, and I reached over to move them. Opal's hands grabbed mine.

"Are you sure?"

"Opal . . . "

Her eyes wandered over the table. "Dammit; I forgot to say goodbye to the place. I forgot I'd never live there again."

She'd scared me for a second with the implication that I had somehow sold her house out from under her, and now I felt a chill of relief as she seemed to accept that it was her own doing. She began to tell me how the bank had twice before tried to take the house away from her. The first time was when Cully's father had just gotten killed on the shrimp boat, and she owed twenty-four out of thirty years on the mortgage. Then, when she got sick a year ago and owed just two years more on the house, the bank tried to foreclose again. That was when she finally called Cully, to whom she'd not spoken in three or four years. Cully told her to go ahead and sell the place as soon as she could and spend the money on herself. He didn't want an inheritance, he said.

"I must be rich," she said, a smile trying to find itself on her uncertain face.

"I think Cully said it went for twenty-one thousand."

Her eyes cast about the sun on the floor as the smile grew, faltered, grew some more. "I was wondering where all that chicken money was coming from. Every time I open my pocketbook, there's all this money. I guess Cully puts it in there for me."

*****

I had the time, a quiver of inclination, and an exact faith that the Buick would make it down to Mobile and back. I'd had all the chrome shined and had the whiteness of the body buffed back so that it glinted here and there when the sun hit it right.

"Looks good," she said as we walked toward the car, arm in arm, Opal's step slow but unwavering. "It was a classy car back when I bought it. Real classy."

As we drove, she told me all about Mobile: hurricanes where shingles, small trees, and parts of billboards blew through the yard; nights camping on the sand with huge fall bonfires and stolen beer; sailors she went dancing with when she was a teenager (having snuck out of the house) and how her father had put her in a closet once and nailed it shut for the whole weekend when six sailors came looking for her one night after her dad had let her out to go to a football game. But Opal didn't care about a football game, or much else her high school friends were interested in; she wanted to go dancing at the bars down in the port. The last sailor showed up at three in the morning. That was when her father woke her up and put her in the closet. She said she spent most of the night feeling around in the dark, trying to decide which clothes hanging in the closet she might have the best chance of permanently wrinkling by lying on them.

She'd been sitting right beside me, her hand on my knee as usual, and most of her weight against me.

"May I put my arm around you?" I asked.

She guided my arm to where she wanted it to rest across those bony shoulders, then shifted her hip back against mine.

"I used to be beautiful," she said nonchalantly. "I don't mean to brag on myself, but it's true. Ask Cully to show you a picture of me. If he's still got one. He might not. I've got some down yonder at the house." She squeezed my hand a little tighter. "I got a nice soft bed down there. Not like that brick Cully makes me sleep on. We can get a good night's sleep tonight." She said it as if she'd offered me nothing more than a glass of tea.

We stopped in Evergreen for Hardee's cheeseburgers. She had me pull over first so she could get in the back seat and pretend I was her chauffeur when we pulled up to the drive-through window. The big black woman who took the money smiled with dismay as Opal railed and mildly cussed at me for not stopping at exactly the right place by the window. I watched Opal in the rearview mirror as she turned to the Hardee's woman with a distraught expression.

"You just can't find good help these days," she said.

When we were out of sight of Hardee's, I pulled over to let Opal get back in front. She was thoroughly amused with herself. "Did you *see* the look on that colored woman's face? That was so funny it made me hungry."

Opal unwrapped a cheeseburger and held it up for me to take a bite. She was about to take a bite too, but she stopped and looked at me. "You mind? I ain't got nothing. Just dead kidneys and a heart condition. No crud I know of."

"Help yourself."

She took a small bite, chewed a long time, finally swallowed. "I just wish we'd thought to get you a cap before we pulled in there like that," she said.

She seemed to remember something and her body jerked a little. She turned on the radio and moved the dial slowly through the static. "Want to hear the Auburn game? They're playing Tennessee. Gonna whup their ass, too." She suddenly recoiled from me with a look of mild horror. "I hope you ain't a Tennessee fan."

"What if I am?"

She took my arm from her shoulder, set it back on my lap and moved a foot away. "I'd be *terribly* disappointed in you."

We laughed. She put my arm back around her. "It's going to be chilly tonight," she said after a few moments. "We'll put on three, four blankets and snuggle up real good."

She baffled me the way she talked about her house, and I wondered if she was just kidding with me or if she really was losing her mind. I imagined her young, imagined her touch as quick and weightless as it was now. I imagined holding her, that narrow skeleton that seemed to have almost too much life right now. I squeezed her shoulder and gave her a quick kiss on the hair.

"Sounds great," I said.

"I know the perfect place," she said. "I used to go there with my favorite boyfriends. Down on Dauphin Island, right on the water. It used to be just twelve dollars a night." She covered her mouth with her hand and looked at me. "I'm telling you all my secrets." She was quiet for a few minutes, staring down at the floor rather than out the windows. "That's why Cully and me don't get along. I was always too wild for him. He said I embarrassed him." Then she threw her head back and sniffed loudly. "Ummmm. Smell them pine trees. We in God's country now." She winked at me. "And He shares a bit of it with the devil.."

She started coughing when Auburn went up by ten. I told her not to be coughing like that until Tennessee came back. She slumped against me, just barely breathing once the coughing had settled down. "Pull into the rest area just down yonder," she whispered, each word slow and labored but distinct.

Just south of Evergreen, I pulled into the rest area. Opal's cough quieted as she glanced around at the cars and the people in their shorts and at the trucks in the distance.

"This is where I used to kidnap my favorite boyfriends to," she said. "I always liked rest areas. It was private in a way, but you stood a good chance of getting caught, too. Made it exciting."

She was quiet for a few moments, and I wondered if she'd fallen asleep. "Need to use the ladies room?"

A slow smiled stretched across her pale lips. "I ain't pissed in months." She still lay against me, lighter by the second, it seemed.

"Let's drive," I said. "Get you to a doctor."

"Let's don't. Just sit here with me."

So we sat. Each time she wheezed that weak cough, I started to put the Buick in gear, but she touched my hand and shook her head no. "It hurts when they poke at you and mash on you and try to keep you alive," She gathered enough strength to turn her face toward me. "You lucky I ain't young." .

"So are you." I tried to keep it light and pull a smile out of her. "I believe we'd be a bad influence on each other."

"You right about that. My daddy'd a nailed *you* in a closet, too." Her voice was only a notch above a whisper but steady. "You love me anyway, though. Don't you?"

"Kind of. Yeah."

"You're sweet. You can take it back if I get better. I won't hold you to it."

That made us both laugh. "Thanks, but what if I don't *want* to take it back?"

I held her hand and felt it slowly loosen, and eventually the rising and falling of her chest slowed to nothing. I sat with her like that for a half hour, I guess. I had no idea how long it took a person to die, or to turn cold after they were dead. Opal looked so peaceful I didn't want to move, but I knew we couldn't just sit there forever. I put the Buick in drive and headed for a hospital. I figured she'd want to be buried in Mobile, so that's where I drove. I carried her into the crowded emergency room and sat her in a chair, where she looked as if she were asleep. I was glad she wouldn't have a bunch of people pounding and mashing on her. There was a clock on the wall, but I'd forgotten what time we got there. After awhile, a very young, tired looking woman, a medical student, I guessed, finally came over.

"Dr. Strong. She okay?"

"She's dead."

The medical student kind of jerked and acted like she was ready to unleash a buildingful of machinery on Opal, but I put my hand on Dr. Strong's arm and told her Opal was fine just the way she was, and that I'd only brought her to the hospital because I had the notion that it was the starting point for attending to a dead person.

"You filled out any paperwork yet?" the doctor asked.

"No."

The doctor got a bit irritated and glanced over toward the nurses' station. "I guess they're too busy." She went to the window, got a clip board, and handed it to me. "I guess we don't need the medical history part." She felt Opal's wrist, then her neck for a pulse. "How long you think she's been dead?"

"Hour. Kidney failure, probably." I filled out the name and address lines, but I didn't know the rest. I handed the clipboard back to the doctor. "Don't know her Social Security number."

"You her son?"

"Boyfriend." The word made a hard, painful breath stick in my chest before I could head it off, and I felt as if I'd said something important and true. I watched the medical student closely and liked her appearance of non-reaction to the idea that such a hollowed-out ghost of a woman as Opal might attract a man.

"Sorry . . ." the doctor said.

"It wasn't your fault." I took out the card that Cully had left me with the number of his hotel in Dallas. "Could you tell me where I can find a phone?"

SNAKE HANDLERS

for Harry Crews

Me and Jake and Charlie had this job cleaning out the snake cages at the zoo up in Birmingham every Friday night. It wasn't a bad job, since it only took us about an hour and a half each time, and we got paid for four hours. But it ended up being a big hassle most of the time because we'd a been out drinking all night, and we always put it off until the last minute. Next thing you knew, it was six or seven o'clock on a Saturday morning and we hadn't done the snake cages yet. We'd have to scramble around to get it done before the zoo opened at nine.

That's when we'd start to get careless.

One time Charlie, who was a short, fat little guy with greasy hair parted down the middle, thought he had one of the pythons looped in his hook (the stick with a leather loop that we moved the snakes around with), and then he started gawking at what I was doing instead of paying attention to his own snake. The python took a swipe that breezed by Charlie's ear. We all screamed, dropped our snakes, and ran. It musta took an hour for the snakes to calm down—and for us to get enough nerve to go back in there and finish up. We were already stomach-sick and hung over, but we all took a poke at Jake's bottle of Wild Turkey anyway before we could bring ourselves to go back inside the snake house that time.

Jake was the only one of us who made it into college. He had passable grades in high school, and his old man could afford to send him because he owned a paint store. Jake was huge—about six foot four and way over two hundred pounds. If you really wanted to get his goat, all you had to do was ask him why he wasn't on the football team. People who didn't like Jake claimed he was too chicken to put on a football uniform and get out there with guys his own size. Frankly, Jake was not popular. He liked to try to lord it over people, which meant that he spent most of his time around guys who were smaller and, in his opinion, dumber than him.

Charlie and me didn't give Jake much grief about not playing football. He would have cleaned us out. But even with Jake being something of a pain in the ass at times, the three of us had been friends since kindergarten. Back then, Jake was the smallest, but when he hit fourteen or fifteen, old Jake took off and got huge.

Jake was the one who got us the job at the zoo. He knew a little bit about snakes because he had an uncle out in Arizona that was kind of a snake enthusiast, or whatever you call people who fool with snakes a lot. Jake got to go out to Arizona almost every summer while he was growing up, and he'd come back with all these snake stories. They had a rattlesnake roundup every year, and Jake's uncle Raymond usually won it because he'd catch big snakes all year round and fatten them up on his farm so he could turn them loose during the roundup and pretend like he'd caught them in the wild. Uncle Raymond claimed that everyone in Arizona did the same thing, but that he just happened to know more about snake nutrition than the others. He said that the secret was to feed them rats and rabbits to fatten them up, but if you wanted them to get long, you had to feed them old chopped-up garden hoses. Jake loved to tell people that, and sometimes I thought Charlie actually believed it.

Getting the snakes to the roundup was far trickier than getting them grown, Uncle Raymond said. People would show up with their own homegrown snakes in knapsacks or suitcases, and the judges knew right away what was going on. But Uncle Raymond had secret ways of getting the snakes there. Like one time, Jake said, Uncle Raymond put a snake to sleep with ether or something, then stuffed it down his pantleg, thinking the snake would stay asleep just long enough for Ray to get him into the round-up. Then Ray would turn him loose and pretend to catch him. But this one time, Ray was chewing the fat with one of the judges who was an old friend, and Ray felt the snake start coming to life in his pants. Fortunately, the snake was hanging by his tail, so Ray only ended up with a few bites on his ankle. If it'd been hanging the other way, Ray might have been cut short in his career as a family man.

*****

The worst time we ever had at the zoo was the night Jake did not show up. We looked high and low for him—all the bars, his girlfriend's house, his brother's place. We called Jake's house about three in the morning and got his daddy mad as hell. About four-thirty, we headed over to the zoo thinking old Jake would show up eventually. Charlie had already been drunk and sobered up twice that day, once in the afternoon and once that night. Now he was drinking again to get his nerve up in case we had to go in there alone. Personally, I wanted to keep a clear head.

Even drunk, Charlie basically didn't want to go in there. He

kept running his hands through that greasy hair of his and looking more and more worried. I'll tell you, if you ever want to see
someone look worried, ask some guy with glasses and real greasy
hair to muss that hair up a little and then think about cleaning
out a snake house. Charlie was actually a whole lot smarter than
he looked. I mean, he had brains enough to flunk his IQ test when
he got drafted.

I said, "Look, we just go in there, grab the snakes, sweep, and
get out. I've watched Jake hold a snake with one hand and use the
whisk broom with the other. We'll make it real fast."

But Charlie just said we ought to try Jake's house again. I'll
admit that cleaning out the snake cages wasn't the greatest job in
the world. Strictly minimum wage. One of the major disadvan-
tages was that we had to save the sweepings. It would have been a
lot easier if we could have just swept everything out onto the
ground, but we had to save everything for this organic gardening
club in town that paid the zoo for the snake and rhinoceros and
monkey and elephant shit that got swept up. It was a big public-
ity thing for the zoo.

"Think we ought to try Jake again?" Charlie asked.

"Let's just get in there and get it done."

Charlie looked real suspicious, in addition to looking dumb
and worried, and says, "One of us is gonna hold the snakes while
the other one sweeps, that it?"

"Yeah," I said.

"Who's doing the sweeping?"

"I am."

"That's what I thought. I'm waiting for Jake."

I just said that to get a rise out of Charlie. Usually Charlie did
the sweeping while Jake and me held. So I said, "Okay, candy-ass.
I'll hold the snakes while *you* sweep."

That was as much reassurance as Charlie needed to get him
into the snake house. I figured if we both went in, one of us might
get the courage to do something.

The snake cages were built into the walls, and most of them
had an old steer skull or something for decoration, depending on
the kind of snake. Every cage had a fake tree for the snakes to
climb in if they were a climbing type snake, and there were little
pools and Spanish moss for the water moccasins.

There was a little narrow corridor that went in back of the
cages, with a small door to each cage for getting at the snakes. It
didn't leave you much room to work. I went to the utility closet
and got out two whisk brooms and two snake hooks. That got
Charlie going again.

"Wait a minute. I thought I was doing the sweeping."

"Shhhh. You want to wake up the snakes?"

Charlie glanced around and hushed up. Usually Jake came blasting in there, snapping on every light there was and hollering at the snakes to rise and shine—as if they could hear anything anyway. When he got really drunk, he'd go in there and start slamming on the walls and throwing brooms and telling the snakes that if they weren't so goddamn dumb, they would have *evolved* into something useful. Other times, Jake would get weepy drunk and pour his soul out to the snakes, telling them that they were the only creatures on God's earth that understood him. It was pretty sickening to watch. I mean, here's Jake, big enough to swallow an alligator whole, standing around bawling to a snake. The weird thing is that the snakes seemed to like Jake and all his carrying on. I swear they'd stop slithering and perk their heads up whenever Jake started in.

I unlocked the padlock on the first cage, and this musty smell hit me like a truck, even though I was sort of used to it. The snakes usually slept curled around each other, and it was tricky business to get the loop on the end of the pole over one snake's head without getting the other snake all pissed off and squirming around. I got it, though, and stepped back. The snake dangled and squirmed, those old rattles started clacking away. Diamondback. He wasn't too big, only three or four feet, but he felt like he weighed a ton. He flicked his tail right near Charlie's head, and Charlie jumped and swatted at the air with his whisk broom and screamed this choked-up little whimper. It made me laugh.

"Hold this thing while I get the other one," I told him. Charlie looked a lot worse than just his normal worried. I finally got him to take the first snake, and I grabbed the other hook and proceeded to try to loop the second snake. I should have paid a little closer attention to Charlie, because I'd just wrangled that second snake into my loop and was hauling him out of the cage when I heard Charlie whimper once more and collapse behind me. Sure enough, Charlie was on the floor and the snake was loose right near him. I dropped my hook and ran to grab Charlie's snake.

That was a big mistake, it turned out. The next thing I knew, I had two diamond-backs loose on the floor. The one near Charlie was just twitching around, not looking real threatening, but the other one was keeping those beady little eyes right on me. I was cornered. They were both close enough that either one of them could have hit me if I'd tried to reach for one of the hooks. The two snakes writhed around for a bit, then they quieted down. I just stood there shaking.

About that time there was a god-awful racket out by the door, and I heard Jake cussing us out for not coming to pick him up. He stumbled into the little hallway where we were and stood against the wall for a minute, weaving back and forth, taking in the scene with a nasty little bleary-eyed grin.

"You two are a sorry crew," he said. "It's hard to believe that two grown boys like you could get yourselves cornered by a couple of itty-bitty rattlesnakes."

I was too embarrassed to say anything, but one of the snakes started toward me and I forgot about Jake and being embarrassed. I mean, that snake wasn't just writhing around and wishing he was asleep; he was headed right my way. I was about ready to faint like Charlie when Jake's hand came out of nowhere and snatched that snake up by the neck. He already had Charley's snake in the other hand.

"Grab a whisk broom and let's get that cage cleaned out fast," Jake said, all businesslike now. "Friggin' fairies," he added.

I was so happy to see him with those snakes under control that Jake could have called me the Queen of Sheba and I wouldn't have cared. I picked up a whisk broom from the floor and was about to stick my hand in there with the broom when I thought I saw a *third* snake in the cage. I didn't see the whole snake; I just saw his tongue flick by the opening.

"Maybe we should take care of Charlie first," I said.

"The hell with him. He don't know the difference."

"What if he gets sick in here?" I wasn't about to put my hand in that cage with another snake in there.

"We'll clean it up. Start sweeping."

I tried to stall another moment. "Wait a minute. Let me check something." I headed around to the front of the cage to look in and see if there was another snake.

"Where the hell are you going?" Jake stood there with the snakes starting to wrap themselves around his arms.

"Gotta check something."

"You ain't gotta check nothing. Get this cage cleaned out and hurry the hell up. One of these snakes is fixing to pull his head through my hand."

I glanced at Jake's hand. It was true. The snake looked like an old piece of rope around Jake's arm, and you could see that snake pulling back through his grip even though Jake was squeezing real hard. But I wasn't about to stick my hand in that cage until I knew what was in there. I guess the snake must have inched back a little more because Jake started to breathe real hard. Ordinarily I would have gone into a panic and tried to help old Jake, but something ornery got into me just then. He was so damned smart, running in here and calling us fairies, accusing us of letting them two snakes get the best of Charlie and me.

In back of me, Charlie moaned again. I saw he was trying to stand up, which he finally did, but he wove back and forth so bad I figured he'd fall down again. But he didn't. He stood there gawking back and forth at me and Jake, who had his eyes shut tight, gripping so hard on the snakes his face was red and his veins stood out like scars.

That the other snake was pulling its way through his hand, too. All I could see of either one of them was the very tips of their ugly faces. I had a flash of the snakes finally pulling back through his hands and striking at Jake's ears and eyes and nose. He wouldn't be able to shake them off, either. Not the way they were coiled around his arms.

"Help me," Jake sort of ordered.

It was bad enough when Charlie and me got scared in the snake house cause we could always depend on Jake to take care of us, but seeing the terror in Jake's face, and seeing the way that one snake's head was bulging in Jake's hand . . . you just knew that snake was getting mad as shit and thinking what he was going to do to Jake the second he managed to pull through that trembly hand.

"What do you want me to do, Jake?"

"Grab one of these snakes by the neck so I can pull him off."

I touched the snake, but it moved right where I touched it, and the feel of the damn thing moving made me jump back.

"Take it, you candy-ass," Jake yelled, his voice back. "Or I'm going to hold you personally responsible for every bite I get. And when I get out of the hospital, I'm going to personally kill you!"

I was working up the gumption to grab that snake when Charlie stumbled over toward me and looked at Jake with this big grin. Just when I started to reach for the snake, Charlie took a hold of my arm.

"Uh uh," Charlie said. "This is too much fun."

He was right, of course. Here was big, strong, dangerous Jake, town terror, at least in his own mind, standing there trying to make it sound like he was giving us orders instead of begging. I thought of all the times he'd bullied Charlie and me over the years. In fact, I got to thinking about how a lot of people in town would have paid good money to see Jake in the fix he was in.

Jake puffed himself up to look his meanest, but he really just looked more and more pathetic. "*Help meeee!*"

I was wishing more than anything that I had a camera. What

Jake would have paid for them pictures. The way the light was hitting his face, you could see the tears and everything. I guess deep down I always knew there was something chickenshit about old Jake. The way he refused to play football was just part of it. I used to wonder what Jake was like when he got out to Arizona in the summertime and he was around all those bad-ass cowboy types that fooled with snakes. Jake claimed his uncle had more snake bites than I had whiskers. Jake used to come back home in the fall bragging about how many times he'd got bit, and he'd show us these little scars that was supposed to be fang marks. I always suspected that Jake just poked himself with a paperclip so's it'd look like bites.

Jake let out another whimper, and I could see that the snakes was just about through his hands. You could just barely see their eyes.

"Thought you said snake bites didn't hurt none," Charlie said. Charlie ain't the smiling type, but he was smiling then.

"Help me . . . please. . . ."

"I remember one time I was cornered by that damned pit bull mutt of yours, and you just laughed," Charlie said, real calm but *mean* calm.

"This is different."

"No it ain't. You were *eggin' that dog* to bite me. And you just laughed and laughed. Called me a dog biscuit, if I remember right."

"I knew he wouldn't bite you if I told him to get back. This is different."

"I don't know, Jake old boy. I ain't sure it is. And what about that time you shoved Jimmy Clark down the stairs and then told him it was me that done it? I lost two pretty decent teeth over that one. I ain't never heard no apology from you."

"I'm sorry," Jake pleaded.

"How sorry?"

"Real, real, real sorry."

"Uh huh. How about the time Cindy Palmer and me was out in my canoe and you come along in your outboard and tipped us over?"

"That was rotten," Jake said, shaking his head in disbelief. "That was when I was going through my rotten stage."

"I believe I would have got some that afternoon, Jake. Woulda been my first. But no, thanks to you, I had to wait almost three more years."

"I'm sorry, Charlie. I'll make it up to you."

I was getting real nervous now. I started imagining what them slippery old snake heads must have felt like to Jake. I didn't know nothing about the things Charlie said Jake had done to him. You think you know somebody all your life, then you find out stuff you never knew about. I had my own list of complaints about Jake, of course, and watching him sweat it now was more fun than I'd had since high school. That was when Jake did the worst thing to me anybody ever did.

One time in March a couple years ago, Jake and me went skinny-dipping down at the river. It was a cold day, but Jake being the macho type he is, insisted we go for a swim. Well, that water turned out to be *real* cold, and Little Willie did his disappearing act. Jake saw it and just laughed and laughed. *Then* the bastard spread it all over school that I ain't got but a one-inch pecker. After that, all the girls would giggle when they saw me, and all the guys, even the runts, wanted to pick a fight with me, like I couldn't be much of a contest if I had a little dick.

But it went way beyond that, too. Aside from not being able to get a date for the senior prom (or for any other occasion, for that matter), nobody wanted me on their softball team at gym class, the teachers all looked at me with beaucoups of sympathy, and some wise-ass put a handicapped parking sticker on my car. It took me six months to live that down, and even then people kept looking at me strange.

"I think you need to *beg*," Charlie says.

Jake's voice got real weak again. "Forgive me, forgive me. Okay?"

"On your knees, Jake old boy. . . ."

Jake kneeled down, his eyes begging at both of us in a real sincere way, and them snake heads just about completely out of sight. "Please forgive me!"

"How about me?" I put in.

"Yes, you too . . . *please* forgive me. . . ."

"Louder."

"Please forgive me, goddamn it!"

Charlie and me studied him hard for a few seconds. I'm sure it must have seemed like an hour to him. Charlie's got that evil grin, and his eyes are all watered up with pure hatred. I was ready to try to grab the snakes, but Charlie held me back again.

"Nope. Can't quite bring myself to it," Charlie said.

Jake jumped back up to his feet. "I'll kill you!"

"You ain't gonna be killing nobody, Jake."

"When I get out of the hospital, I'll kill you, by God."

Charlie grabbed my arm and pulled me toward the door. "In that case, I guess we better leave now so's we can get out of town."

"No! Wait. I didn't mean that."

I figured Jake must have been feeling them snakes slip some more. He started whimpering again. I tried to think of one good thing Jake had ever done for anybody, and I couldn't remember a single one. I wondered why Charlie and me hung around with Jake, taking abuse from him just about every day for all those years. From the look on his face, I figured he'd learned his lesson.

I ain't sure why I finally made a move, but I did. I grabbed the snakes right behind Jake's hands, closed my eyes, and squeezed. I didn't even breathe. Jake peeled the snakes off his arms while I stood there, squeezing them two snakes' necks as hard as I could. I didn't open my eyes until he grabbed the snakes and heaved them back into the cage and slammed the little door shut.

Jake leaned back against the wall, the sweat pouring down his face and flying off him every time he twitched. In a minute or two, he snapped out of it. He still looked a little shaky, but I could see he was already of a mind to forget what had just happened and be his old prick self again.

Charlie and me glanced at each other, ready to run if we had to. But Jake, a.k.a. Mr. Cool all of a sudden, moved on down the row of cages to the next one, which contained the cobras. The door had a double lock. Jake spat on the floor as he turned the first combination padlock, and he cussed a little as he turned the second. He opened the door just a crack. I thought his face looked real strained and sickly. He just stood there frozen.

I looked over his shoulder. The cobras were awake, and I could see the two hoods bobbing around, ready to bite the shit out of anything stupid enough to show up in that cage.

"I don't think I'm up for this," Jake said. "Let's go home."

"They'll fire us, won't they, Jake?"

"No. We're going to quit first. Soon as they open up. Before they know the cages ain't cleaned out."

Jake didn't want to hang around the parking lot for a breakfast beer like usual. He just got in his old VW bug and scrammed on outta there. Charlie and me looked at each other and busted up.

*****

Jake did the quitting for us, just like he got us the job. Old Jake was pretty humble the rest of the summer, the one time I saw him before he went back to the university. But by Thanksgiving, he was back home bragging all over town about how he was the only guy in the state who knew anything about snakes, and that after he graduated, he was moving out to Arizona to get into snake-handling full time. But like everyone figured, Jake just went to work at his daddy's paint store. He never did go back to Arizona. He still drank, but you never saw him trying to pick fights anymore. I even heard someone saying one night that old Jake had turned out to be a real nice guy after he'd gotten over his wild years.

I went in the army for three years, and Charlie went in the Merchant Marine, after he took another IQ test and passed. Charlie stayed in, but I went back home when my hitch was up. I ran into Jake on the street about a week after I got back, and he seemed glad to see me. He'd put on fifty or sixty, and he moved a little slower than he used to. He showed me pictures of his wife and kid. He was just getting off work, so we went to a bar called The Circus Room. We must have talked for an hour. Before we left, Jake offered me a job at the paint store, but I got trained as a medic in the army, and I figured I could get something better.

"You remember that time you and Charlie were cleaning out the snake cages and two of them got loose on the floor before I got there? Remember that?"

I figured he was leading into the part where we made him sweat over the two snakes that were slipping through his hands. "Yeah? What about it?"

"That kind of taught me a lesson." He didn't say anything for a few seconds, but I could tell he wasn't finished yet either.

"Oh yeah? What kind of lesson?"

"Well . . . it's hard to explain. It's kind of like . . . like I was glad to be there to help my friends out of a jam."

I realized he'd forgot he was in a pretty tight spot himself that night, and I couldn't help but think that was the point he was trying to make—you can look at a situation any damned way you want. Remember the stuff that makes you look good, forget the stuff that makes you look bad. He had me going for a second there, thinking he mighta turned humble or something.

He patted my back. "Well. What do you say? You want to come to work for me? You can start tomorrow if you want."

"Hey . . . I appreciate the offer, man. But I'm gonna take it easy for a few days. Maybe take a month off and just kick back."

Jake got a black look on his face for a moment, and I realized he wasn't the kind of guy you wanted to depend on for something important, like your living. People don't change all that much, even when they think they have.

On the Postcard Road

for Jack Kerouac

*V*ince wasn't sure he could make it all the way from Alabama to Maine in his condition, but he was willing to try it anyway. His brother Brad, ten years younger than Vince, read sports magazines as he waited at the kidney dialysis unit for Vince to finish his treatment. Leaving directly from dialysis would give them two and a half days to get to the treatment center in Maine, where their other brother, Wesley, had arranged for Vince to be dialyzed during his visit.

Brad wheeled Vince in his chair to the car. Dialysis used to leave Vince feeling refreshed, but for the past three months, the treatment only left him feeling depleted, since no machine on earth could purge him completely anymore. He was unable to lift his limp and shortened left leg into the car, so Brad had to reach under and guide the lifeless leg inside. Vince spread his elbows like wings to support himself on the car roof and the top of the door while his left leg was being set inside. Then he dropped himself onto the seat, wincing but trying his best not to groan.

They were planning to stop overnight twice along the way so that Vince could rest. There would be few, if any, bathroom stops for Vince, since his kidneys had shut down more or less for good. Brad had brought a grocery sack full of gauze and bandages for dressing Vince's wounds—the gaping crevice where Vince's hip had been removed, and the sores all over his back and buttocks where waste fluids that were not removed during dialysis built up under his skin and eventually burst through. Vince's stomach was prone to vomiting, he was hard of hearing, and he was almost completely blind, after suffering a stroke of the optic nerve during the winter. He was young, just fifty-three, but his body had buckled under the hard life to which Vince had subjected it.

Nor was Vince slipping gently into his dark night. Each new sore or scrape or shaving cut caused in him an alarm that would have been ridiculous in a man who was comfortably far from his end. With Vince, mere inconvenience became calamity, and even minor pain became yet another chapter in his long purgatory.

Brad knew the trip would be hard on Vince, but Vince had

talked all winter about how he wanted to see Maine once more. Now that he was blind, he said he wanted just to smell the coast— the ebb tide and the fishing boats and the sardine cannery where he had worked—one last time before he died. And to taste fried clams, whether they made him sick or not. Everything made him sick now, so why not have it be on something that tasted good.

Brad got in on the driver's side. "How do you feel?"

"Awful. My ass is sore and my hip is killing me."

"Sounds fairly normal."

"Let's just go."

For the next fifteen minutes, Vince described in great detail the difficulties of his treatment that morning; they couldn't get the dialysis needles into the shunt in his right leg because the leg was so badly swollen. Then the lines kept clotting, his leg cramped during the last half hour, and finally they had trouble stopping the bleeding when they pulled out the needles because they'd had to use blood thinner to overcome the clotting. Vince's blood was already thin enough, he often told people. Any thinner and it would turn into steam.

Brad tuned out the tirade, as he'd learned to tune out most of Vince. It occurred to him now that Vince had him captive for two or three days, and that it would be impossible to go into another room or go out to visit a friend so that he could get away from Vince's self-absorption and perpetual state of alarm. Brad started to settle into a bad mood, but the motion of the car soon put Vince to sleep. Brad hoped the sleep might last all the way to Virginia, where they would stop for the first night.

But Vince, his head on his chest and his toothless lips in a creased bulge that touched both his chin and his nose, died before they reached the Tennessee state line.

Brad had been absorbed in his own thoughts, but when he glanced over at Vince, he knew by the slumped posture and utter stillness that Vince had slipped away. Brad felt a powerful and unexpected chill. He pulled over into the breakdown lane along the side of the interstate, and for several minutes he studied his brother's corpse. It was slumped forward with only the seatbelt holding it up. Brad sensed its emptying, like the deflating of a thin-walled ball. Finally he reached over to touch Vince's chest. No sign of breathing or heartbeat. Vince was gone.

There was a choice to be made: drive back to Birmingham and contact an undertaker, or drive to Maine and find an under- taker there? It seemed an easy choice. Brad had always planned on burying Vince in Maine, as close as possible to their mother and father. Why not save the cost of transporting the body in a hearse, or a plane, or however they were likely to ship Vince?

For a year, Brad had peered each evening into Vince's room when he came home from work, wondering if he would find Vince in that final stillness. He recognized that he longed for it at the same time that he longed to see Vince triumph and prosper and hang on until ninety. There would be a little insurance money and the restoration of freedom, and also the end of Brad's resentment. He considered his resentment of Vince a normal and natural thing which would be unnatural to deny. But he also tried to balance that resentment with a showy cheerfulness when he was actually performing—changing dressings, half-carrying Vince down the stairs for visits to a sizable list of nephrologists and orthopedists, or wheeling him around the grocery store while Vince proceeded to buy one of everything on every shelf. Every inch of cupboard and refrigerator space at Brad's small apartment was already full of Vince's whim. That sort of resentment could now go the way of all past resentments. But best of all would be the end of Vince's pain. He was glad that Vince's light had gone out like a candle in a breeze rather than a bulb exploding.

*****

As he drove through Chattanooga, Brad noticed a new smell in the car and realized that Vince's body had ridded itself of its last few hours of metabolism. The smell was something he hadn't counted on a half hour before, when he decided to keep driving. A friend of his in Birmingham claimed that out in the country fifty years ago they would embalm a body with brake fluid if they were planning on a home burial. Vince would love that, Brad thought, as crazy as he had been about cars all his life. But embalming was not the question. Getting Vince cleaned up and seated in a better position before rigor mortis set in were the questions that Brad had to address soon. He hoped a shower in a motel would deodorize the corpse sufficiently to make the trip bearable. He also wished it were nighttime so he could get the corpse into a motel room without being noticed, but he realized that any motel would have floodlights that would make what he had in mind even more conspicuous at night than it would have been in broad daylight. He'd have to find a small, uncrowded motel to get it done. He began to study the signs along the road for motels without national chain names. He drove over twenty miles to make sure he was well outside of Chattanooga before he saw a sign for Sunset Paradise Motel. It was one-thirty, and Brad figured Vince had been dead less than two hours.

He parked far enough from the office to keep Vince out of sight. To his relief the parking lot was empty. The motel manager

was a middle-aged Indian or Pakistani woman who seemed uninterested in the registration card Brad filled out. She was totally
placid until she announced that Brad owed her thirty-two dollars
and fifteen cents. Then she smiled, as if she might invite him to
dinner in the next utterance.

"I hope you enjoy your stay here, Sir."

"Thank you. It might be short. We just want to rest a bit."

She looked hurt. "Not stay the night? Why not?"

"We'll see." Brad left the office quickly. The car was starting
to smell strongly now, and Brad gagged in the heat and the stench.
He drove to the room he'd been assigned. It was in the middle of
the motel. He had thought about asking for a room at the far end,
but he was afraid such a request might have aroused suspicion.
Instead, he would be in full public scrutiny as he attempted to
move the corpse into the motel. Brad unlocked the room and went
inside to inspect. He pulled the curtains shut and checked the
shower. Then he went back to the car to bring in his suitcase. He
laid out a change of clothes for himself, then tried to decide how
he should dress Vince. How would Vince have wanted to look for
his last ride? Would he have dressed casually, semi-formally, or in
his favorite pajamas? For the past year, Vince had favored one set
of flannel pajamas, but it was summertime now. Flannel pajamas
would be out of season. Brad remembered a bright yellow polo
shirt Vince had picked out for himself just before he went blind—
and had worn frequently thereafter. But Vince had never played
golf in his life, and a polo shirt just didn't seem right. Brad decided instead to dress the body in the one suit he had brought
along for himself. It was his best suit, but Brad decided the occasion demanded his best suit. He could always buy another.

He also had the presence of mind to bring in one of the plastic garbage bags they'd brought along to dispose of car trash. When
he had everything laid out on one of the double beds, Brad went
back to the car to bring Vince in. Vince had never been light, and
now he was heavier than ever. And slipperier. Brad had hoped to
carry the body gracefully, but he ended up having to grab it around
the chest from behind and drag it. He got Vince into the room,
then kicked the door shut. He wanted to stop long enough to
taste his relief, but the smell of shit clouded the room. He wrestled
the body across the floor and into the tiny bathroom with its
peeling walls. It was good, he thought, that the place was a bit
run-down; he wouldn't want to shower a corpse in a Hilton.

By the time Brad got him into the shower, Vince's shirt was
wadded up to his chest and both slippers had fallen off. The left
sock was nearly off. Brad realized that the corpse did not com-

plain about the roughness the way the living body had, wrenching with pain just to have its bad leg lifted into the car. Even so, Brad tried to be gentler. He lay the body in the shower, then yanked and tugged to get the clothes off. The smell and the sight of the smeared body finally got to Brad, and he knelt at the edge of the toilet to throw up. His eyes watered and his stomach muscles wadded up painfully as the vomit flew from him. When he was done, he took a deep breath and settled back against the bathroom wall.

After he'd rested a few moments, he glanced at Vince, who lay in an inhuman heap in the bathtub, his toothless face mashed against his chest. He staggered to the bathtub and wasted no time in pulling off the rest of Vince's clothes. Those that didn't come easily he ripped off. Then he stuffed the soiled clothes, his and Vince's, into the plastic garbage sack.

Before he got into the shower with Vince, Brad collected all the washcloths and threw them into the tub. He studied his brother a moment. *Don't think of him as Vince—just think of him as something that needs to be washed and repackaged in a hell of a hurry.*

Brad got into the shower with Vince. He pulled the curtain inside the tub, turned on the water to the right heat, then peeled the paper wrapper from the splinter of soap the motel had provided. The shower was instantly a cloud of steam. He knelt on the floor of the tub to start the washing, four wet, soaped washcloths draped over his hand. The water alone was washing off most of the crud, and Brad worked quickly to remove the rest with the washcloths. He was rough in turning Vince, but he reminded himself that this was not the time for wasted tenderness. It took all Brad's strength to lift Vince up for the rinsing. He turned Vince as best he could, then hauled the wet body with him out of the shower, leaving the water running. He half threw, half hoisted Vince onto the empty second bed.

He grabbed all the towels he could find and dried Vince off, then sprayed him heavily with deodorant and sprinkled after-shave lotion all over him. He fashioned an enormous diaper from the two bath-sized towels and secured it by tying the ends of the towels. He had some trouble pulling the suit pants over the towels, and getting a shirt on Vince was even harder, since he found himself trying to avoid wrinkling it. He smoothed the shirt roughly, then buttoned it to the neck, and finally wormed a red necktie under the button-down collar and tied it. He sat Vince up to jostle him into the suit coat, then lay him back down. Socks, red ones to match the tie, and shoes, Brad's own loafers, went on much more easily. Brad stood back to admire his work, even though the body seemed to shrink inside the suit.

He went to turn off the shower, then dried himself and put on fresh clothes. He brought the plastic bag to the dumpster and brought everything else back to the car. Before he moved Vince, he left a ten-dollar bill on the dresser with a note that said, "For the towels I took." He set the room key beside the money, then added to the note. "I'm sorry we couldn't stay longer. Please don't take offense. I'll be sure to recommend your motel to any of my friends who may be passing through Tennessee."

*****

With the corpse bathed and deodorized, Brad cruised through East Tennessee toward the Virginia state line. He stopped for gas at what seemed the least crowded service station along a stretch of truck stops, where no one seemed to notice either Brad or his passenger.

He got to Knoxville during the rush hour. As Brad waited in the standstill traffic, he tore a pillowcase into strips and tied Vince's head to the headrest so the body would not stiffen with its head on its chest. He fished around in the back seat to find a hat he could put on Vince to conceal the strips of pillow case that held his head erect. There was only an old golf cap. Brad decided it looked elegant.

The traffic was light between Knoxville and Bristol, and Brad glanced often at Vince. The body was riding well. Brad was satisfied with his performance in getting Vince cleaned up and into riding condition, but now the fact of Vince's death began to settle over him as the early evening light grew dim toward the east. Life would be very different without Vince. It would be more private, a few thousand dollars richer, an entire world freer. Brad had told himself that when Vince passed on, he'd take himself a long vacation in Mexico or in the islands. Perhaps he'd be able to talk his boss into letting him take a month-long leave of absence.

Brad glanced at Vince and smiled. Maybe he should take Vince on a cruise instead of just bringing him home to Maine to bury him. Bodies could be preserved. A taxidermist could probably stuff one. Why not just keep old Vincent around as part of the family? Sit him up on the couch in the living room and dust him off once in a while. He could be a real conversation piece.

The thought of conversation made Brad feel guilty again. Conversation was the one thing he had not been able to give Vince during the past year. Vince's only topics of interest lately were his hip, his shunt, his blindness, and the sores on his back and behind. When Brad could listen to no more, he usually found an excuse to leave the room or the apartment. Sometimes, when he didn't feel like leaving, he'd try to steer Vince to a more bearable topic, such as a recounting of all the times he'd lost his driver's license. Vince had had driver's licenses from ten different states, he claimed, and had had each one revoked. He'd not held a license in over twenty years, but that did not prevent him from driving, at least not until he lost his hip three years ago.

Another topic toward which Brad would sometimes steer him was all the cars Vince had owned. He claimed to have owned over eighty cars. Brad doubted that, but he listened to the stories anyway, or at least pretended to. The car stories were better than the dialysis stories. Brad thought about the many times he'd snuck out of a room and left Vince talking to himself. Or the times he'd pretended not to be in the apartment when Vince called for him. Brad thought he could tell when Vince wanted something truly important by the tone in his voice. If it was not important, there was no sense in revealing his presence, since Vince would often ask for things he could have done for himself. While Vince slept or listened to the TV, Brad felt a bit of freedom. He was not free to play his stereo or cook something in the kitchen, lest he draw Vince's attention, but he was free to stay in the living room or out on the balcony. Vince occupied the bedroom. Brad slept on the couch. In a way, Brad had felt freer since Vince lost his eyesight because Vince couldn't tell if Brad was at home unless Brad announced himself. He rationalized such hiding by telling himself he was there if Vince had an emergency. But more than once Brad had listened to Vince crying softly to himself in his bed that he was all alone.

"I'm with you now, Bubba. I'm sorry about leaving you alone the way I did, but I'm kind of a loner. You always hated solitude but I love it. I need it." *And now I have it back,* Brad thought.

He noticed the bad smell again and wondered if Vince had eliminated some more, or if the smell signaled the onset of decomposition. It was only eight o'clock. He knew he had at least fifteen more hours to drive. He reached across Vince's lap to roll his window down, then rolled down the back windows, too. The breeze took away most of the odor, and Brad smoked one of Vince's cigarettes to counter what remained. He could stop in any town and turn the body over to an undertaker, he reminded himself. In the fleeing light, Vince's fingers looked shrunken, and his fingernails protruded far over his fingertips. With his head tied to the headrest, Vince's jaw was slack and his mouth hung open. Brad wondered if the odor was coming from the open mouth and he tried to think of a way to close it without having to stuff something inside. He could think of nothing.

As he pondered, a piece of tread tore loose and hammered

against the right rear tire wall. Startled, Brad quickly slowed and pulled over. It occurred to him that he should roll up the car windows in case someone stopped to offer help.

He had forgotten to check his spare before leaving Birmingham and was relieved to find it usable. He wrestled Vince's wheelchair out of the trunk to get at the tire. He took out his jack, popped off the hubcap, and began loosening the lug nuts. Behind him he heard a car pulling over into the emergency lane, and when he turned around, he saw it was a state trooper. His heart began to belt against his ribs, and his breath was short and feathery. *This is it,* he thought.

"Got it under control?" the officer asked. He was young and terse. Brad had the impression that what this cop hated most about his job was having to appear friendly.

"Yessir. I believe so. If this jack works." Brad continued to work, hoping the officer would go on his way.

"This road's kinda dangerous. I can turn on my lights until you're finished."

"That's okay. If the flat was on the left side I might need your help, but . . ."

"I'll turn them on anyway."

In a moment, the blue and white lights were knifing at the dusk. Brad worked as quickly as he could. The odor from the corpse came and went faintly. Brad worried that the officer might smell it, but if he did, he said nothing. The officer bent near the tire holding a flashlight so Brad could see better. *Keep the beam right there,* Brad thought, his hands shaking as he pulled the flat off and lay it on the ground. The officer seemed absorbed by the process and held the light beam transfixed on the vacant wheel well. Brad hung the new tire on the lugs, spun the nuts on as quickly as he could, then jerked the jack lever to lower the car. He frantically tightened the lug nuts and pounded the hubcap back into place with the heel of his hand.

"Y'all set?"

"I think so." Brad wrestled the flat and the wheelchair back into the trunk. "Thanks for the help."

The officer eased back onto the road and coasted by Brad's car. *He sees Vince,* Brad thought darkly. *And now he's going to pull over and ask me what the hell I'm doing with a corpse.* But the cop accelerated instead.

*****

Brad drove on into the Virginia night, by Marion and Pulaski. Somewhere an hour or two above Roanoke was the half-way point, but he was still at least two hours from Roanoke. Once again he had timed the ride through southern Virginia very poorly. He was always there at night, missing the gentle mountains and small farms nestled among the green and golden hills of the post cards he saw in truck stops.

The whole route was like that, passing through the least populated part of Alabama, in the Appalachian foothills. The Shenandoah Valley in Virginia, the coal mountains of Pennsylvania and West Virginia, the khaki rolling hills of grass in Southern New York. *A postcard road,* Brad thought, picturing.

The encounter with the cop amused him now that it was over. An older cop might have understood, but not a young one.

"A close brush with the law, Bubba," he said to Vince. "It would have been the morgue for you, the slammer for me."

Vince's body seemed to have slid closer to the door while his head remained tied to the headrest, as if he were trying to escape from the car. Now Brad felt energized and ready for the all-night jaunt to New England. He speculated on timing. He'd get to Scranton around daybreak, just before the traffic got bad. Then to Binghamton for rush hour. By the time he got to Albany it would be late morning, then he'd take the Mass Pike east and skirt Boston on 495. He would avoid bad traffic in any one place as long as he kept covering ground at this pace.

"We're gonna get there, Bubba. Just try to keep the B.O. under control and we'll have you in a nice comfortable coffin in no time at all."

Maybe this *is* a sacrilege, he thought. Brad had not considered himself a member of any religion since he was fifteen, but this was the sort of thing that would have offended his parents' religious convictions, was it not? He'd acknowledged more than once during the past year that the reason he'd taken Vince in was because his parents would have expected it of him, had either of them been alive. Brad visited Vince in a nursing home in California six months before Vince came to Alabama. Brad was appalled at Vince's life in the nursing home, where Vince, only fifty at the time, looked every bit as old as the truly aged. It was the first time Brad had seen his brother in five years. A nurse directed Brad to a small room, where people were herded to chain smoke for the hour or so that smoking was allowed each evening. Vince's social worker had tried to warn Brad that Vince looked bad, but Brad was still unprepared for the old man he saw at the end of the table, puffing away in a haze so thick that the people in the room were barely visible.

Later, when he wheeled Vince back to the room he shared with two wizened men who lay in their beds mumbling to themselves, Vince spoke softly about how he'd like a room of his own but couldn't afford it on his pension.

Brad took a motel room a mile away and came back for another visit the next morning. "Look, Bubba, we've got to get you out of here."

"Like where?"

"Alabama."

"With you?"

"Yeah."

"How the hell are you going to take care of me?"

"The hard way, I guess."

"I'd rather just go to an old soldiers' home."

"You ain't old and you ain't a soldier anymore, Bubba."

"What's this *Bubba* business?"

"That's what we call folks in the South."

"Thanks for the warning."

As soon as Brad got back to Alabama, he began trying to avoid the obligation he'd taken upon himself. He didn't return calls from Vince's social worker, he lost applications for nursing homes in Birmingham, and he pretended that Vince would probably die before the proposed move to Alabama. But it didn't happen that way. A few months after he saw Vince in California, the body arrived, alive, in Alabama.

Brad was a few minutes late getting to the airport. He found Vince in his wheelchair by a baggage carousel, his two canvas suitcases at his side. Brad knew from letters and Polaroid photos that Vince, only two years earlier, had lived in a double-wide with furniture-type possessions and a dog named Bear. Now he owned only two partially torn suitcases.

"You found me a nursing home yet?"

"No. Thought you could stay at my place."

Vince barked a hard, short, unsmiling laugh but said nothing.

"Glad to have you here," Brad said.

Vince gave the wheelchair a deft spin and headed toward the exit, leaving the baggage with Brad. "We'll see."

Brad adjusted as he always did when he had no choice. He gave Vince his bedroom and began sleeping on the couch. Taking care of Vince seemed easy at first. Vince cooked for himself, got himself in and out of the bathroom, and seemed fairly content to watch television alone in the evening. He also changed the dressing on his hip by himself. An ambulance picked him up to bring him to dialysis and back home three mornings a week. The government paid for everything through Medicare, and Social Security paid him a monthly disability pension. Vince insisted on paying a hundred dollars a month for rent. Brad let him.

Since his expenses were next to nothing, Vince had money in his pocket for the first time in several years, and he wanted to spend it. The weekly trips to the grocery store were grueling for Brad, who hated shopping anyway. Now he had to carry ten or twelve sacks of groceries up the stairs and find space for everything in the small cabinets. Brad spent far more time than he wished in check-out lines of grocery stores and K-Marts. Vince quickly filled the apartment with cheap radios, polyester clothes, shoes he never wore, tape players, three TVs. Vince usually slept during the day and roamed the kitchen and living room in his wheelchair at night.

So Brad started spending nights with old girlfriends he didn't really want to see. At forty-two, he'd been divorced three times and had sworn off serious involvements. He had taken it into his head to learn to play classical guitar, and that was how he tried to spend his free time. He was already pretty good, after three years of obsessive practice, but now it was difficult to play at home. Vince would wheel himself into the living room and wait for a pause in the music. "Jesus . . . I had a rough treatment today."

When Vince's hip got badly infected, playing the guitar became impossible for Brad. Vince lay in bed moaning, sometimes gasping or crying out when he tried to move and the pain stormed down his leg and up his body into his head. After a week, the infection ebbed, and Brad again spent his nights away. He always left Vince a phone number where he could be reached, but he spent only one or two nights at home each week.

Sometimes he saw Beth, a woman he'd met in the office where he used to work. They had had a brief affair while they were both married. She had two small children and a blatant desire to rope them a new father. She was attractive, dark-haired and dark-eyed, eager to please, very domestic, the kind of woman he would have married ten years earlier. Beth was also religious and claimed that having sex outside of marriage made her feel guilty. She did it anyway, of course, but the aftermath was always heavy on Brad. He came to accept that sleeping with her without sex was the best approach. But then she seemed hurt. He knew he didn't want to marry her, so he stopped seeing her and slept on the couch at home for a month.

Then he started seeing Anne again. She was blond and sparkling, with eyes that were soft and hazy when she smiled. He liked Anne, and at times thought he could fall in love with her if he let himself. She was lively, intelligent and easy to talk to, but he knew she was seeing at least two other men. He felt uncom-

fortable and depressed whenever he thought about her other rela-
tionships. He always felt obliged to call first to make sure she was
alone before he went to sleep with her. He stopped calling her
altogether after she put him off for a week while an old boyfriend
from California visited.

Through his guitar teacher, Brad met Cleone, who was a nurse.
She usually worked the all-night shift, so she and Brad would spend
the evening together before she went off to work, leaving Brad an
empty apartment in which to sleep. But he didn't much like
Cleone; she was too rough in bed. She was also a complainer, a
country girl who had spent her entire adult life trying to divorce
herself from her background. She had acquired the most superfi-
cial trappings of a snob, and she constantly criticized other people's
taste in clothes and cars. Brad surmised that she'd taken up music
lessons only so that she could tell people she was learning to play
classical guitar. But she had no idea who Vivaldi was and had
never heard of Julian Bream or Andres Segovia. He tried to help
her practice, but she was clearly not interested in learning, and
her clumsiness with the guitar infuriated Brad. He came to
Cleone's apartment later and later each evening, sometimes waiting until she had left for work, letting himself in with the key she
had given him and leaving in the morning before she got home.
One evening he found a note asking him to leave the key when he
left the next morning.

So it was back to the couch. Brad considered finding a bigger
apartment, but he hated the prospect of moving. Brad once again
patted Vince's thigh. The combination of corpse odor and after-
shave was getting worse, and they hadn't even reached Roanoke.

Brad tried to tell himself that guilt was trite at a time like this
and he tried to think of the vacation he would take. He tried to
think of the white clothes he would wear in the islands, and the
pastel drinks he would consume in the afternoon, after he'd prac-
ticed on the guitar for five or six hours. He would eat brightly
colored food all day and consume pastel drinks from noon until
bedtime.

Drinking had become a problem for Brad during the past year.
He showed up at work with frequent hangovers that left him limp
at his desk. He was a customer service advisor for a computer
software company and spent his work days on the telephone talking to people whose computers wouldn't do what they expected.
That the problem was the expectations, not the computer, never
occurred to them, Brad had noted for years. Ninety percent of the
calls would have been unnecessary if the customers had first looked
in their user manuals. But they always called as their first step.

On mornings when his hangover was particularly severe, Brad would come close to telling his customers they were idiots. And this from a guy who had once been considered a perfect service advisor because of his patience and sense of humor. Now Brad despised his job and found most of the people he worked with small-minded and boring. Being a tad blasted in the evening made it easier to seem cheerful while he was cleaning Vince's hip wound and changing his dressings. And Vince, who had finally quit drinking when he started dialysis treatment, insisted on paying for Brad's beer. It was Vince's way to drink vicariously, Brad figured.

He reached into Vince's shirt pocket and pulled out another Lucky Strike. The cigarette needed coffee and the car needed gas. Outside Harrisonburg, in northern Virginia, he saw signs for a truck stop and exited the Interstate. Again he rolled up the car windows, even though the idling diesels that filled the lot spewed their own powerful odor. A bearded attendant in a John Deere Tractor hat stood near the car waiting to collect Brad's money. Brad could see that the guy had noticed Vince.

"Your buddy looks bad. He sick or something?"

"Sleeping."

"There's a hospital about four miles up the road."

Brad came close to telling the guy that what Vince really needed was a nice cozy hole in the ground, but he decided not to make the guy think too much. "He just needs to rest."

Back on the postcard road, Brad drank coffee and smoked cigarettes and felt energized for another hour. By the time he reached Winchester, he'd drunk all of the coffee and smoked six more cigarettes. He recognized the failure of yet another attempt to quit smoking, which was to be on this trip. He'd managed to quit for two years before Vince came to live with him, but Vince's three or four cigarettes a day were too tempting, and Brad caved in and began smoking regularly again after three months with Vince.

The stench was getting stronger, and Brad decided he had to stuff Vince's mouth after all. As he drove, he rummaged in his suitcase in the back seat for a handkerchief, causing him to swerve. In moments, headlights appeared behind him, almost in the backseat. The car pulled out beside him and cruised by, slowing so as not to pass. Brad recognized it as a police cruiser, an unmarked one. The cruiser's lights went on, and Brad, his heart storming, pulled over. This time he didn't have time to roll up the windows. He scrambled out of the car to meet the officer.

"Everything all right?" The trooper was hatless and white-haired, and in his glasses he looked almost like Brad's father.

"Yessir. Just looking for a handkerchief. Allergies."

The officer sniffed, and one side of his mouth twisted upward. "Damn. Something smells bad." His flashlight beam settled on Vince's sunken form. "That guy alive?"

Brad knew he was trembling too badly not to look guilty. "No, sir. He's dead. He's my brother. I'm trying to get him home to Maine to bury him. We were headed there on vacation when he died."

The trooper looked at Brad's license and registration. "How you stand that odor?" the trooper asked.

"Keep the windows rolled down, spray him with deodorant every hour or so, keep the fan on high and the vents pointed straight at him. Keep reminding myself he's my brother."

Right then Brad felt the officer let him go. "I believe you a good family man," he said, handing back Brad's paperwork. "Hope y'all make it to where y'all tryin to git to."

*****

Brad's emotions sharpened as dawn broke in the eastern sky. He knew he still had a hard drive ahead and wasn't sure where he'd find the energy, now that the Virginia state trooper had gotten him thinking exhausting thoughts. He couldn't stop in a rest area because the odor would attract attention, and he couldn't try to sleep with the windows rolled up because he'd suffocate. Stopping on the road would attract a cop.

Brad began to cry. He cried for the pitiful life Vince had led, for the pain and disappointment Vince had caused their mother and father, for the many times Vince had slept on park benches, or in missions, or in VA alcohol treatment centers, or in jail. He cried for Vince's excruciating year in the hospital after his accident, in which Vince was knocked down by a truck and run over by three cars before anyone had brains enough to pull him out of the road. With no insurance, Vince was shuffled from one hospital to another over a period of five weeks before anyone tried to treat his injuries. Then the orthopedists had to rebreak his bones so that they could mend correctly, knowing, unlike the believing body on their table, that they could never really fix him.

Brad remembered a term—throw-away lives—that came up in a discussion with some people in his office about the homeless. Vince had just come to Alabama a few weeks before, and Brad was still full of the pride he had taken in himself for opening his home to this vagrant brother who had never held a job more than a few weeks, never maintained a marriage for more than a few months, never attempted to support or know his four children, and had lived on one government pension or another for nearly twenty years. A classic non-contributor.

Brad tried to tell his coworkers that there was no such a thing as a throw-away life—not in the sense they thought. An individual might choose to throw his life away, but it was outrageous of a society to presume to make such judgements about the lives of its members.

"That's right, you've got your brother living with you now, don't you? And somebody said he's real sick?"

"That's right."

"Boy, I'll bet your life has changed."

"Yes. It's much better."

"Get real. . . ."

"I feel honored to help my brother when he's helpless."

Brad now hated his hypocrisy and self-righteousness. He did, in fact, consider Vince's a throw-away life. But he was not planning to be the one who threw it away.

"I didn't throw you away, Bubba. Sometimes I wanted to, but I didn't. I did your laundry and took you shopping and carried your soup into your bedroom so you wouldn't spill it in your wheelchair. God damn it! I did what I was supposed to."

Brad caught himself ranting and quieted down. He'd done all right, he told himself. He knew he had been far from perfect, but he had done what he could. He hadn't really given Vince a place to live so much as he'd tried to give him a more pleasant place to die. It was realistic. It was not sentimental or maudlin or callous. It just was.

They were in Pennsylvania now, and Brad realized he hadn't even noticed going through the tiny strips of West Virginia and Maryland. He'd traveled this road a dozen times and knew when to expect the crossing of each state line, but only the Maine state line seemed important this trip. In the new sunlight, Vince looked bad. Anyone who saw him now would know for sure that he was only a remnant.

Brad noticed a speed limit sign that said fifty-five. He was going seventy-five. Yes, a speeding ticket and a cop who might be a lot less sympathetic than the one in Virginia. Brad turned on the radio. He hated popular music, but it was the only thing that came in clearly. His stomach rumbled and he realized he had not eaten in nearly twenty-four hours, but his mind could not get past the odor inside the car. The thought of embalming Vince in brake fluid entered his head again. Instead, he picked up the can of deodorant and sprayed the bundle of clothes and its head for the fourth time.

When he stopped again for gas, just before crossing into New York State, he bought more deodorant and a nose block, as well

as some sandwiches, cans of soda, and a thermos full of coffee.
The sun was already hot, and now he faced directly into it as he
turned east toward Albany. The nose block made a big difference.
He was able to eat without gagging, and his eyes didn't cloud.
Whereas he had constantly studied Vince's form during the night,
now he kept his eyes away.

*****

Between Binghamton and Albany, Brad had trouble staying
alert. What finally slapped him awake was a sign that reminded
him the Massachusetts Turnpike was a toll road; he'd have to stop
at least twice to deal with toll booth attendants. The odor was
unbearable now; even with his nose blocked, he could taste it and
feel it. Any toll booth attendant would catch that scent and immediately notify the state police. He considered alternate routes,
but he knew of none that would be as fast as the turnpike.

When the first toll booth came into sight, Brad pulled over to
roll up the back windows and gave the body a good long shot
from the new can of deodorant. He reached over to roll up Vince's
window, and his arm touched the bloated belly. Brad thought for
a moment he would lose his sandwich, but he didn't. He stopped
only long enough to grab the toll ticket from the attendant's hand,
then accelerated. He didn't think the attendant had noticed anything. That meant he was safe for awhile. A mile beyond the toll
gate, Brad pulled over to roll down the windows again. He felt an
irritating sense of relief over having passed such a simple obstacle.
Getting off the pike and having to pay would mean a longer stop.
Unless he had the money counted and ready.

His energy returned as he thought about how close to home
he was. Just two small states away. But with toll booths in all of
them. The one in New Hampshire would be an automatic toll
booth; all he needed there was to throw in his coins and go. But
on the Maine Pike, he'd have to deal with attendants again, unless
he wanted to drive up Route One. But Route One in the summertime was like a convention of Maine state police. If he got to Maine,
he wouldn't care if they caught him. He'd be where he was trying
to go. Brad lay the gas pedal a little closer to the floor. The speed
limit was fifty-five, but all the Massachusetts types were going
seventy. Growing up in Maine, Brad had always felt that Massachusetts was a foreign country. He remembered many childhood
trips to Massachusetts, and as a child he'd assumed the state was
just one continuous turnpike full of cars whose occupants basically wished they could be in Maine or Vermont or New Hampshire. Anywhere but Massachusetts.

Knowing that he was near enough to home that getting caught

was no longer important, Brad got more daring. He saw a sign for fried clams and decided that was exactly what he wanted.

"Your usual?" he asked the corpse, without looking at it.

He pulled in at the Howard Johnson's, went inside, and ordered fried clams, knowing they were far from the real thing. The air-conditioning made Brad want to stay an hour or two in the Howard Johnson's—until he noticed he could still smell the corpse. After he placed his order, he tried to stay apart from the other people who were waiting for their take-out orders. When his clams were ready, Brad went back to the car. He wondered if he should eat the clams first and then get in the car, or get in the car, put on his nose block, and eat the clams while he drove. He got into the car, put on the nose block, opened all the windows, and tried not to smell anything until the car was in motion and he'd built up a good breeze.

Eventually he remembered the clams on the seat beside him. He ate one, then forgot about the others. Instead he thought about Anne and wondered if her guest had gone back to California yet. Or if Jack, her weekend boyfriend, had gotten the job he was interviewing for in Oklahoma City.

As Brad neared the turn-off for Interstate 495, he began to worry that any attendant with a fraction of a functioning brain would smell the corpse, look inside the car, and immediately notify the police, who were often stationed near the turnpike exits anyway. Brad pulled over to the side of the road to think before he traveled any farther. He baked for several minutes beside the road until the stench of the corpse drove him from the car. He could see an exit with high-rise service station signs staring off in either direction about a mile away, but they did not mean anything until a black Mercedes pulled into the emergency lane just ahead of him. Brad trotted toward the car.

"Out of gas?" a white-haired man asked.

Brad realized that if a wrecker were to haul him off the turnpike, he could roll up the Chevy's windows to block the stench, pay the toll attendant, and be on his way.

"No, sir. I'm out of engine."

"I have a phone. I can call the Exxon station up ahead and have them send a wrecker."

Brad tried to think of something to say to acknowledge the man's kindness, but he could only nod, which made the sweat drool down his neck.

"Send a wrecker for a bronze Chevy," Brad heard as the Mercedes coasted away.

The wrecker was there in minutes, driven by a young guy

with dark hair and eyes and a bored expression. He had come from the opposite direction, and cut across the median into the northbound lane. He jerked the tow truck around as if it were a toy.

"Whatsa problem?"

"Need a haul."

Brad had not closed the windows, even though he saw the mechanic's face glaze for a moment as he caught the odor. His eyes went straight to the front seat.

"Holy shit! Is that what I think it is?"

"A dead body? Yep. That's what it is."

"No shit. D'jou bump him off or just find him?"

"Just found him. I thought I'd bring him home for the kids to play with."

The mechanic hacked a loud laugh. "You got some weird kids, mister. So, where do you want to haul this thing?"

"Just off the turnpike."

"Hey, man. This ain't a taxi."

"I'll make it worth your time. But let's get it done before the cops spot that body." Brad got into the wrecker. As they drove, the mechanic kept asking questions about the corpse. He seemed disappointed when Brad told him the real story.

"You mean you drove that thing all the way from Alabama stinking like that?"

"It didn't stink until Tennessee."

They got through the toll booth as easily as Brad had hoped. He gave the mechanic twenty-five for the service call and twenty-five more as a tip.

"Look, do me a favor, will you? Don't mention this to anyone for an hour or two, okay? Let me get out of the ungodly state of Massachusetts, then you can tell anyone you want."

The smile returned to the wrecker driver's face. "Sure, man." He unhitched the Chevy, and Brad headed out.

Since the car had been closed up in the heat for ten minutes, neither the nose blocks nor the cigarettes Brad smoked could defeat the odor. He felt as if he'd left Alabama a week ago rather than twenty-two hours ago. But once he was on I-95 headed toward the New Hampshire line, Brad hardly remembered the exhaustion he'd felt at daybreak. He was almost home, and the Chevy hummed along, in spite of the fact that the engine rap was noticeably louder than when he left home. He decided he would leave the car in Maine, fly home and buy another car back in Alabama. The Chevy wasn't worth an engine job, and the smell of the corpse might never go away.

Passing over the bridge from New Hampshire into Maine, Brad got his first whiff of the ocean. The cool salt smell cheered him for a moment and made him think of the ice cream his father used to make on the porch on Sunday afternoons.

"Remember that, Bubba?" But Brad's mind soon switched back to the mode of choosing the best route for the last two hours of the trip. He opted for Route One, rather than deal with any more turnpike toll booth attendants. But at the first stoplight in York, he wished he had taken his chances on the turnpike. The odor from the Chevy seemed to fill the whole town, and the slow pace of the traffic was maddening. In Kennebunk, traffic was backed up for a quarter of a mile, and pedestrians winced and complained and moved a little faster as they crossed the street or walked along the sidewalks. A few seemed to recognize that the stench was coming from the Chevrolet, and they pointed toward Brad with disgust. He thought of his Alabama license plate and laughed as he realized that he was adding to the state's bad name.

But soon his thoughts again turned dark, and a new surge of guilt pulled at him. What he had intended as a dignified ride home for Vince was now just a desperate clawing at the highway with Vince as unwanted, repulsive baggage. It was like throwing up all over yourself, then showing up at church to get married. Brad kept his eyes on the cars in front of him and tried to appear unaware of the problem he was creating. His eyes burned and his unsteady stomach bubbled. He gave the body another shot of deodorant, but that only made Brad gag.

The idea of driving anyone else from Alabama to Maine in death would never have entered his mind. But with Vince, it had always been different. With Vince, the more preposterous the better. And Vince leaped at every chance to make a fool of himself, like an old rejected dog groveling for any attention he could get from anyone who'd give it to him.

There were also the few moments in Vince's past when he had been more than only a buffoon. Brad remembered one time when he was no more than seven or eight that Vince rose to the level of hero. Brad came home from school complaining that Russell Allen's brother had built Russell a go-cart, and that Vince and Wesley never built Brad anything. After supper that night, Vince went down cellar to their father's workshop and built Bradley a small desk and chair.

Brad counted the miles—just sixty—before he'd arrive in Bridgton. He circled Portland toward the lakes region. He counted the miles and the hours behind him and recalled Vince's words when the prospect of traveling first came up.

"Going to the supermarket half kills me. How the hell am I going to make it all the way to Maine?"

Brad had taken the warning lightly, figuring that death would be a deliverance for a man who had suffered as much as Vince had. But now Brad thought of himself as someone who had made the decision he claimed to revile, the decision to throw away another person's life. He jerked himself out of that train of thought and tried to notice the trees and the small towns along the road instead. Everything reminded him of Vince. There was a small dance hall where Vince used to go on Saturday nights when he was just out of the service. And there was the causeway in Naples where you could rent a ride in a speedboat or in a plane with pontoons. Brad pointed out all the old sights to Vince. He was just ten miles from Bridgton now. Anything he did, no matter how fatuous or melodramatic was all right if it helped subdue his guilt. The guilt was from fatigue, Brad decided. It was understandable, wasn't it?

He thought about his apartment and how he wouldn't have to move after all. He'd throw out the bed Vince had used; it was stained almost solidly with blood and betadine and hydrogen peroxide that had been spilled as they changed Vince's dressings. He'd hire a maid to clean the place, and he'd get the walls painted where Vince's wheelchair had scraped and left permanent black marks. He'd have to return the wheelchair and the walker and the taped programs for the blind and the special recliner and all the other equipment, most of which Vince had never used, to the various agencies that had issued him these things. And he'd inform the people from the church who came to visit each Sunday morning that they no longer had to come. The visiting nurses and ambulance drivers had turned the small apartment into a hospital ward, and Brad looked forward to seeing no more of them. He'd have to remember to notify the government to stop sending the pension checks. There was a lot to do.

*****

On the outskirts of Bridgton, Brad stopped at the first telephone booth he saw. First he called the undertaker who had buried his mother and father, then he called his brother, Wesley.

"I'm uptown," Brad said.

"You're a day early."

"Just couldn't get here fast enough."

"You must have driven straight through."

"Straight through. Yes."

"How's Vince?"

"Better."

"Well, come on down."

"I can't just yet. I thought I might ask you to meet me at the funeral home."

"Funeral home? Ahh . . . that's what you mean by better?"

Brad realized the odor of the corpse was everywhere, but now the repelled faces of the summer people coming out of the supermarket in their shorts and sandals amused him as they looked around, wondering what it was that smelled so bad. He wished that Wesley had accompanied him on the trip. They could have drunk together and given Vince an Irish wake of sorts. A rolling one. They could have told each other Vince stories. A clown's eulogy. Brad had a whole new slew of them. Like Vince's bedroom wall at Brad's place. Vince insisted on keeping up his subscription to *Playboy Magazine*, even after he couldn't see anymore, and each month Brad would ceremoniously tape the current centerfold to the wall in parade with the last.

"What's she look like?" Vince would ask.

So Brad would describe the model in minute detail, including the lighting, the color and angles of her sculpted pubic hair, and the degree of either innocence or wantonness of her lips and eyes. Vince would lie there with a big smile. He claimed he hadn't had an erection in five years or more, but he liked to think about the centerfold women anyway. Less than a minute into the description, Vince would get very serious, his face startled with recognition. "Wait a minute. What's her name?"

"Sandy Moorehead."

"She blonde?"

"Yeah. I already told you that."

"I know her. She was a waitress at this place I cooked at in Chicago, fancy place."

"Matter of fact, that's exactly where she's from."

"*Sandra*. She was a beautiful girl."

"Still is."

And Vince would drift off into the time he knew her, and with that big grin, he'd start to tell Brad all about the time they spent together, right down to the wrenching break-up. It would be a fifteen- or twenty-minute story. But Brad would be long gone, out on the balcony smoking or playing his guitar to himself while Vince recounted every searing moment of what had been one of the great romances of the century. Vince had always let the young ones go. For their own good, he used to say.

A BIT OF SOPHISTICATION

For Erskine Caldwell

Craig was already late for his date with Mylinda-Anne when his right front tire blew out. He swerved in the sand at the edge of the pavement and almost plummeted into the gully beside the road. Once he'd managed to bring the old Plymouth to a halt, he turned off the engine and sat a few moments, recovering. As his trembling subsided, he became aware of the sounds of the night—the owls, the crickets, the frogs, the crackling of the engine. He'd owned the Plymouth only one week and could not remember ever opening the trunk to see if there was a jack, let alone a spare tire. When he got out to look, he was right—no spare. Neither did he have a flashlight. He felt around in the dark trunk and found parts of at least three jacks, although he wasn't sure he had a complete one. He lit one match after another until he'd assembled what seemed like a workable bumper jack.

When he saw that the jack would, indeed, lift the car, a new worry beset him: he would have to stand in the gully to loosen the lug nuts. He assumed that the gullies were full of snakes, and that he'd be taking an awful chance, getting into the gully with them. He hoped the lug nuts were not on too tight, but they were, and as he struggled with them, he sensed that snakes lurked no more than two feet from his ankles.

He'd finished loosening the lug nuts and was jacking the tee-tering car up to pull off the tire when the sound of a roaring engine rose in the distance. Craig knew the rear-end of the Plymouth was not quite off the pavement and that the car had come to rest midway through a long curve in the road. The sound of the engine grew, and he realized that it was two cars, not just one. Two idiots racing, he thought. Then he saw the glow of a flashing blue light through the trees. A speeder and a cop. When they came around that bend, they were sure to ram the Plymouth.

The headlights burst into view, and Craig leaped feet-first into the gully, snakes or no snakes. The first car blasted past, spraying the bushes with sand as it skidded and screeched but missed the Plymouth. A moment behind, the police car roared by, its blue light whirring like a propeller. The angry engines thundered until they grew fainter and finally folded back into the night.

Craig, shaken and dry-mouthed, crawled out of the gully. His feet were wet, his underarms clammy, his breathing fast and terrified. Leave the car, walk home, and come back to take care of it in the daylight, he told himself. But two things forced him to attend to the situation immediately. First, he had been unable to get the Plymouth inspected, since the floorboards and rocker panels were rotted out, the brakes were shot, and the windshield had an enormous spider-web crack. Two or three hundred dollars worth of work on a car for which Craig had paid only one hundred and twenty. So, he'd had to improvise on the inspection sticker. The new sticker was green—S&H green, Craig decided—and he remembered that his mother still kept a box of the old trading stamps somewhere. A square of sixteen stamps was also the right size. He couldn't leave the car by the side of the road with an inspection sticker made of S&H Green Stamps. Not if he ever wanted to see the old Plymouth again.

But it was the second reason that drove him as he finagled the heavy tire free of the car and started down the road to the filling station he'd passed about a mile ago. This was not just a date; it was a date with Mylinda-Anne, the most beautiful girl he'd ever seen in person. She and Craig had just graduated from high school a month ago, and, as luck and the alphabet would have it—they had the same last name, Drake—they had marched side by side in the procession. She smelled like flowers, whereas the other girls smelled like perfume. She had genuine blond hair, eyes so brown they were almost black, and a fetching tilt of the head when she took his arm and looked up into his face at graduation practices and said his name, drawing it out in her Southern accent.

"Ca-*ray*-ig, Honey, I don't have a zit coming up by my nose, do I?" Or, "Ca-*ray*-ig, don't you just love the watch my Paw-paw down in Mobile sent me for graduation?"

It wasn't until graduation practice that Mylinda-Anne had noticed him, and when he invited her for coffee afterward, he was astounded that she said yes. Over coffee, they talked about everything from the difficulty of adjusting to a new home, especially such a cold one, to how much she missed Mardi Gras, crawfish, barbeque and Buffalo Rock ginger ale, her favorite drink. They became telephone friends, talking for an hour or two almost every night. Craig noticed that with him, the Southernness of her accent was barely discernible, unlike the exaggerated *y'all* and *fixing to* and *Lord have mercy* he constantly heard from her at school.

It had taken all the nerve Craig had ever owned to ask her out for coffee after that first graduation practice, especially since she

was already attached—to Carlton Potter, no less, who played football, basketball, baseball, captained the wrestling and golf teams,
and was All-New Hampshire in almost everything. He was going
to Northeastern on a wrestling scholarship. But Carlton and
Mylinda-Anne had a stormy relationship whose main feature was
break-ups and reconciliations. They were currently broken-up,
Mylinda-Anne told Craig. And this time she hoped it was for good.

All the girls at school despised Mylinda-Anne. They despised
her accent, which they insisted was completely put on. They despised her being named head cheerleader when she'd been in the
school only that year. They gossiped about how the male teachers, not to mention the boys, drooled over her. Mylinda-Anne,
they said, did the unthinkable; she put out. And although they
acknowledged that Mylinda-Anne was not the only girl in the
school who put out, she was odious in that she seemed to think
she was better than the other girls who put out just because she
got good grades. But Mylinda-Anne got good grades, the rumor
went, because she put out to the teachers.

The fact was that Mylinda-Anne really was smart. Her father
was a Shakespeare scholar on the faculty at UNH, and her mother
taught sociology. Between them, they could afford the outlandish
tuition at Dartmouth, where Mylinda-Anne would go in the fall.

So Craig, who'd been consumed for a week by her yes when
he asked her out on a date, trudged along the dark country road
lugging a flat tire, having barely escaped from a gully full of snakes,
and having been spared dismemberment, if not death, at the hands
of a maniacal driver. But he felt powerfully that his travails would
turn out to be worth all the effort before the night was over.

*****

The filling station was around the next bend, and Craig wondered if he should call Mylinda-Anne to tell her he was going to
be late. No; that would give her an opportunity to tell him not to
bother. She did have a bitchy side, he knew from the many and
long phone conversations. When he saw the Texaco sign still
lighted, he walked faster.

The station attendant, a kid Craig did not know, sat behind
the counter in his soiled Red Sox hat reading a girlie magazine.
His face was flecked with a light stubble, making him look like a
twelve-year-old hobo. He did not look up when Craig walked in
or when he spoke.

"Can you fix a flat?"

"Ain't got a mechanic at night."

"You don't have to be a mechanic to fix a flat."

"Then fix it yourself."

"Look, I don't know how to work the machine. Just fix it, will you? I'm late."

The kid's face grew a mean smile. "Ten bucks."

"To fix a flat? Three."

"Ten bucks."

Craig knew he had no choice. The next station was five miles back toward town.

The kid took his time, spitting on the floor and cussing a lot.

Craig went into the men's room to try to clean up. His white shirt and jeans were smeared with tire dirt, and his shoes were soggy and scum-caked from jumping in the muddy gully. He washed his face and hands, then pulled twelve paper towels from the dispenser to carry the tire with. He looked in the mirror. There just wasn't anything as disgusting as a dirty white shirt. After he picked up Mylinda-Anne, he'd go by his house to put on a clean one.

"Hurry the hell up, will you?"

The kid glared at Craig and told him to go pound sand up his ass. When he was finished fixing the tire, he demanded twelve dollars instead of ten. "For harassing me to death," he said.

Craig paid him the twelve. That left only eight for the rest of the night. Getting into a dance would take six. Maybe she'd settle for coffee afterward. Or just a Coke.

His arm ached and he'd managed to sweat through his already filthy shirt by the time he rounded the bend where his car was parked. He was so consumed with his thoughts that he didn't notice the police car pulled up in front of his own until he was less than twenty yards away, at which point the officer turned on his blue light, stepped out of his car, and flooded Craig's face with his flashlight.

Craig's stomach flashed in unison with the blue light. No registration, Craig thought. A fake inspection sticker. Fifty dollar fine for each of those. Probably jail for the night. On the other hand, the lack of registration could be a good thing. Craig made an instant decision to keep walking.

"Hey! You!"

Craig stopped and turned around. "Yessir?"

"This your car?"

"Nope." He started to walk again.

"Hey! Hold it right there! Don't play games with me. This is your car and you put those green stamps on the windshield."

Craig trembled as he replied. "Nope. Not my car."

The flashlight crawled down Craig's front, then back up to his face. He could only guess how furious the cop must have looked.

"I wanna see your license and registration."

Craig lay the tire on the pavement and fished out his wallet. He opened it to the slot where he kept his license. The flashlight beam bore in on the license as the cop came nearer, then back at Craig's face.

"I couldn't tell you about the registration," Craig said. "Not my car."

"Then where you going with that tire?"

"Home."

"Home? I know everybody that lives out this way. I never seen *you* before."

"Craig Drake, Sir. You know . . . the Drake family."

"Never heard of them."

Craig figured that if the cop didn't know Mylinda-Anne's family, he was bluffing when he said he knew everyone. Her mother and father would have cringed to hear Craig say he was a member of that family. The one time he'd met Mylinda-Anne's parents, he'd spilled hot chocolate on Ms. Drake's cashmere sweater and told Mr. Drake that the state should lower the drinking age to eighteen again.

The flashlight beam dipped from Craig's face to his hand. "If this isn't your car, what's *that* for?"

"I left the tire to get fixed this afternoon and figured it'd be good exercise to walk back for it instead of driving."

The cop opened the back door of the cruiser and motioned Craig inside. "Why don't we just take a little ride to this place and you can prove to me that you have a car there waiting for a tire."

Craig sighed and got in the cruiser.

"And hold that damned thing on your lap so you don't get my car all dirty."

Inside the car with the cop's face in the mirror glowing in the dashboard lights, Craig saw that he was young, maybe twenty-five, and had a thin, hard face. As they drove, Craig tried to fashion two stories, one for the cop and one for Mylinda-Anne. As far as Mylinda-Anne was concerned, his chances would vanish the instant he showed up in the back of a police cruiser. But he still had to deal with the cop.

"This tire isn't for a car in my yard," Craig ventured. "It's for a friend of mine who lives back in town."

The cop laughed. "Hell, I should have figured that's what you were up to. I must know ten, fifteen people walk around on a Saturday night with their friends' tires."

It was silence after that. Three miles from where the cop had picked Craig up was the Drake place. Craig directed him between two granite pillars. A long driveway curled through the pine trees that abruptly opened upon a vast, dark yard. There in front of Mylinda-Anne's enormous stone house sat Carlton Potter's red Trans-Am. A stereo bellowed from inside, and the house seemed almost to throb.

The cop's face brightened. "By God . . . there's the son of a bitch I was chasing a while ago. I lost him when I almost hit that Plymouth back there." The cop glared at Craig in the mirror. "*Your* Plymouth, I still believe."

The cop jerked the cruiser into park and jumped out.

"I know that car," Craig volunteered.

"Oh yeah? Whose is it?"

"Guy named Carlton Potter. Better be careful. He's dangerous."

The cop smiled. "He better be, cause I sure as hell am."

Craig watched the cop scamper toward the house, drawing his night stick as he mounted the steps. He rang the doorbell and stepped to the side, his back against the wall. A porch light came on. The door opened. When Mylinda-Anne, in only a short, terrycloth bathrobe and a towel wrapped around her hair curlers, saw the cop, she shrieked and ran back inside. The cop followed.

"You can't come in here when I'm dressed like this," she screamed.

A booming male voice also ordered the cop out of the house. The cop and Carlton Potter shouted at each other, and above their voices, the shrill, soprano voice of Mylinda-Anne Drake sang a single-note scream.

Craig wrestled the tire out of the car and lay it against the trunk of the maple tree in front of the house. Cursing and crashing and Mylinda-Anne's screams mixed with the screeching electric guitar music on the stereo. Craig climbed to a low branch of the maple to watch through the window. Inside, the cop had shoved Carlton up against a wall while he put on the handcuffs. The whole left side of Carlton's face was bleeding, and Craig guessed the cop must have slugged him with his stick. Mylinda-Anne watched, her hands sometimes at her cheeks, sometimes over her eyes. When the cop led Carlton outside, knocking the screen door back against the wall as they stumbled through, Craig climbed higher in the tree. The cop shoved Carlton into the back of the cruiser, smacking Carlton's head on the roof of the car. More shoving and cursing. The cop finally crammed Carlton in the car and slammed the door. He looked back at the house.

"Where's that other jerk? The one with the tire?"

Mylinda-Anne turned on the floodlights and stood in the doorway, her hands still up to her face. "What jerk with a tire?"

"Never mind," said the cop. He got in the cruiser and sped out of the yard, spitting gravel from his tires. Mylinda-Anne continued to stare. After a few moments, Craig swung down from the tree and alit beside his tire. Mylinda-Anne let out another small scream, then looked at Craig with what seemed a great fatigue on her cold-creamed face.

"Oh. So you're the jerk with the tire. . . ."

Craig raised his hand. "Right here."

Her eyes roam tiredly over him, coming to rest on his smudged shirt. "Ca-*ray*-ig, Honey, you look like you been rode hard and put up wet."

They laughed as they both gazed toward the driveway once again. Beyond the thick woods they could see the glow of the flashing blue light above the trees. Then the siren started, and they listened to the fading sound.

Mylinda-Anne sat down heavily on the porch steps and shook her head. "I *swear* . . . I thought that cop was going to bust Carlton's head wide open."

"Good. He damned near killed me the way he was driving." Craig reflected on how his flat tire had been a fortunate occurrence. Otherwise he would have been here with Mylinda-Anne when Carlton showed up.

"Don't be ugly," she said.

"I thought you two had broken up."

"Well, you know how Carlton is. He wanted to talk it over one more time." She smiled. "Especially when he heard I had a date tonight. I reckon he probably wanted to tell you not to try anything *fresh*."

Craig could not conceal his annoyance. "You told him you had a date with *me*?"

Her smile held steady. "I guess that wasn't very smart." She looked him over and a small frown brought her eyebrows together. "Anyway, you're late."

"And you don't exactly look ready to go out to a dance."

"Well, I was just fixing to get into a nice warm bath when that awful drunk, Mr. Carlton Potter, showed up at my door."

"I see. . . ."

"It's a good thing my Momma and Daddy weren't home, don't you think?" She stood up suddenly. "Listen here. Maybe you should come inside and take a shower while I throw those clothes of yours in the washer, you hear?"

*****

It was more than Craig could have wished for: Mylinda-Anne at home in just a little blue terrycloth robe, her parents at a concert in Boston for the evening, and Carlton Potter behind bars, at least for the night. Mylinda-Anne led Craig inside the house and up the stairs to the bathroom. Still grasping his arm, she looked deep into his eyes.

"Now, Hon, if my parents happen to come home early while you're here, you're going to have to exit through that window over there, shinny down that tree, and disappear, whether your clothes are finished washing yet or not. You hear?"

"Sure."

"I'm serious. Now. I'm going to stand outside in the hallway here, and you hand me those dirty clothes." She backed out of the bathroom, pulling the door partially closed.

Craig considered opening the door wide to hand her his dirty clothes but held himself back. Instead, he cracked the door open and handed her his shirt, pants, socks, shorts.

She glanced at the shorts, which were dark red bikini style, and grinned. "Cute," she said. "Now *hurry*. And dry yourself *inside* the shower, not out. So you don't get the floor all wet."

Craig found the shower the most luxuriant he'd ever had. He washed himself all over with a thick, clear shampoo that smelled like strawberries. He found a brush with which to scrub the dirt and grease from his hands and under his fingernails, then he shaved, just so he could use a pink plastic razor there in the shower—one that he imagined Mylinda-Anne used to shave her legs and, perhaps, trim her private hair for her bathing suit. His erection was insistent, seemingly permanent, and he rolled it roughly between his soapy hands.

He dried himself inside the shower stall, as he'd been directed to, threw the towel over the shower curtain rod, then put on the robe that Mylinda-Anne had told him he'd find in the closet. It was a long, red velour robe—her father's, Craig guessed. He used some green mouthwash he found by the sink and brushed his hair with a pink brush that he also assumed to be Mylinda-Anne's.

He carried his sneakers down to the living room where he found Mylinda-Anne, still in the same short robe that came half way up her thighs. The cold-cream was gone, but she still wore the towel and curlers, which made him think she had no intention of going anywhere. She sat on the couch, her legs crossed, one heel raised, as she smoked a cigarette and blew the smoke toward the ceiling. Craig thought she had the longest, palest, slenderest neck he'd ever seen. Her knees were beautiful, as were her red toenails—and the way she held that one heel high off the floor was the most tantalizing thing he'd ever seen in his life. He was glad the robe he was wearing had pockets so that he could conceal the true measure of his enchantment.

She smiled. "Much better. Have a seat."

He sat in the middle of the couch so as not to crowd her and yet be in striking range, in case she said or did anything that seemed inviting. Without the stereo, the only sound was the busy chugging of the washing machine.

"Well . . . here we are." She looked at him with a quizzical smile, her eyes darting about his face and hair. "I'm just not sure just what to do with you."

He slid a little closer, hoping she wouldn't move away. Instead, she took his hand and held it.

"What do you *really* think of me?" she asked.

"I think you're cool."

"Cool. What does that mean?"

"I think you're great."

"Great."

"Yeah."

"How so?"

"Just that you're terrific."

"Craig, Honey-pie. You're not being very specific."

His heart beat faster as he tried to find words that would flatter and impress her. "Well . . . I know this might sound strange, but I think I'd like to marry you."

"Aha! So that's what cool, great, and terrific mean?" She stubbed out her cigarette and moved closer to him. "May I kiss you?" she asked.

Rather than answer, Craig leaned closer to her. Their lips met lightly and inertly at first, as if they were both holding their breath to see what would happen next. Then their lips grasped each other more firmly, feeling their way around as far up as her nose, as low as his chin and back again to lips. Her tongue lurked just behind her slightly open lips, and he let his own tongue touch hers for a quick moment to see what she'd do. When he tried to go deeper, she pulled back until it was only their lips again. The breath from her nose was warm on his cheek and chin.

She withdrew, still holding his face, and looked at him. "That was very nice," she said. "You're a sneaky one."

"Sorry."

"I guess I kind of led you on." She patted his knee and moved back to her corner of the couch. "I was just curious." Her smile lingered like her lips. "So, you let me kiss you. Is there anything you'd like . . . from me?"

Craig spoke before he could find reasons not to. "May I feel you up?"

She laughed and looked away, suddenly shy. "I don't think so. That's getting a bit intimate, don't you think?"

At that moment the washer stopped, and Mylinda-Anne jumped up from the couch. "I'll be right back," she said.

Craig waited impatiently, but he did his best to appear cool, casual, unfrenzied by her sensuous kiss, which was the best he'd ever had. She was back in moments. The intent sound of the washer was replaced by the much gentler and more soothing whir of the dryer. To his disappointment, she sat in the chair opposite him rather than on the couch.

"Tell you what," she said. "I can't let you touch them, like you want to, but . . . maybe I'd let you *see* them. . . ."

Craig's heart knocked itself all over his stomach as he tried to wheeze out a yes.

"This is because you're my friend," she said, her face grave and admonishing. "I'd never do this with my boyfriend." She paused. "Think of it as kind of like being at a topless beach down in Mexico, on in France. Men don't jump all over a woman just because they can see her breasts. . . ."

"Right," Craig said, in barely a whisper.

"I've been around a little bit," she said. "And I don't just mean around *here*." Mylinda-Anne sat forward, toes firmly planted on the floor and heels raised and let the robe inch down over her shoulders. She stopped it just above her breasts.

"This is a test, Ca-*ray*-ig darling; can you look only at my eyes, even when my breasts are showing?"

"Sure. Of course. . . ."

"We'll see." She let the front of the robe fall open until both breasts stood out bare and unflinching as she stared at Craig, who feared most of all that she'd cover herself again if he looked directly at them. He forced himself to look only at her eyes, even when she reached for a cigarette from the arm of her chair and flicked her Bic to light it. She blew the smoke at him.

"Well? Do you think I'm sophisticated?" she asked.

Craig thought he knew what sophisticated meant—something about sipping wine and looking at paintings in a museum, or going to operas and speaking foreign languages, or eating weird things and claiming you liked them. Now he wasn't completely sure what sophistication meant.

"Sure," he said. "Very." But he could stand it no longer; he had to have a full, photographic look, something he could commit to memory, and he let his gaze wander downward. They were more pointed than rounded, and the veins spread and wandered almost like the blue lines on a road map, just under her skin.

She did not cover them when he looked, nor react in any other way. "So," she sighed. "I feel like I'm the one doing all the talking here. Tell me about yourself."

Craig lifted his eyes back toward hers. His heart flitted like a flat little stone over a lake. "I'm just kind of normal."

"Like me?"

"Yeah. Exactly."

Mylinda-Anne pulled the robe back up over herself, and although she smiled more expansively, a sense of loss crept over Craig like a light rain. Neither spoke, and Craig wondered if he'd really seen what he'd just seen, or if one of his ridiculous fantasies had intruded. He forced himself to smile back.

"So . . . I guess this means you won't marry me?" He hated himself even as the words escaped, carelessly molded and hardly sophisticated, from his lips. He was grateful when she laughed.

"No . . . but thanks for the offer."

"Do you think you'll marry Carlton?"

She really laughed now. "That mama's boy? He couldn't leave this place. The man I marry will have to live in the South and learn to like grits and okra and the Word of God on a hot Sunday morning."

Craig had never heard of grits and okra and was afraid to ask.

*****

They talked awhile longer, mostly about who at school was a bitch and who wasn't; who among the guys was a loser and who was okay. Craig was glad that she didn't put his name up for evaluation in that regard. He listened more to the dryer than to Mylinda-Anne, hoping the dryer would go on all night. When it stopped, he thought for a moment that she shared his sadness.

She glanced at her graduation watch. "Well . . . my folks'll be coming back any time now. I guess you'd better run."

He followed her into the laundry room, where she handed him his clothes, an item at a time, shorts last. He remembered when she'd seen them upstairs and had called them cute. She was more businesslike now. Craig decided to be sophisticated, too; and he let the robe fall to the floor and dressed in front of her, one sock, another sock, his shirt. Rather than put his shorts back on, he pulled on his jeans and stuffed the shorts in a front pocket. He put on his shoes, but stuffed the laces inside rather than tie them.

"That was very good," she said, taking him by the arm again, smiling as she led him to the door. They pecked on the last step of the porch. As Craig walked by the Trans-Am, he nearly buckled under a wave of envy. Carlton was mildly crazy, the way girls liked a guy to be. He had a great car, a great summer job coaching basketball for eighth-graders. Plus he was mildly smart, mildly tough, mildly handsome—overall just too damned possibly perfect for Mylinda-Anne. Craig was a busboy at the UNH Student Center, waiting to go to the community college and learn how to become a motel manager. He and Carlton Potter were not just in different leagues, they lived on different continents of possibility.

He stopped by the Trans-Am, took out his pocket knife, and began to scrape. "Tell Potter I'll pay him for this. He can get another one easy enough."

It was a ragged job, but it was a real inspection sticker. Craig started down the driveway but got only three steps away when he stopped and went back.

"Almost forgot my tire."

She laughed, which made him feel like a fool rather than an entertainer, and the laughter followed him all the way back to his car, like a breeze in the trees. To his great surprise, the Plymouth had not been hauled away. He put on the tire, then licked Carlton Potter's inspection sticker and held it against the S&H Green Stamps on the windshield until it stuck enough to get home.

Craig was pretty knocked-down for a couple of days, thinking about his evening with Mylinda-Anne and how nothing could ever come of it. When he didn't feel depressed he felt angry, and he quit his busboy job and took another one pumping gas at a filling station. He tried to read a novel, the first book he'd ever read without being ordered to, but he could not concentrate.

Mylinda-Anne called him late the third night and wanted to know if they could still be friends, at least until she went off to college in the fall.

"I've got *boy*friends," she said. "But I don't have hardly any friends."

"Sure," he told her. They talked until sunrise and had coffee together that afternoon. She told him she hoped he'd come visit her at Dartmouth some weekend. He told her he would, but only if he didn't have to talk to anyone. She said she thought she could arrange that at least once, but after that he'd be on his own.

THE FRIENDS OF THE TREES

for Robert Penn Warren

*I*t was already dark, and an icy moon hung in the bare branches of the maple trees, floating there like an old balloon from last summer. The smell of the paper mill was faint and only intermittent in the razor bursts of breeze. Jerry stood under a street light on the corner, holding his jacket closed at the neck and watching his breath float upward, toward the moon, the way he used to when he was a child. He'd forgotten his gloves, and his hands were red and a little numb. He told himself he'd put out flyers on one last street and then go home.

When he knocked at the door of the first house, a porch light come on above him, and the shadow of a bent old woman came to the gauzy curtain over the glass door but did not open it.

"Who is it?"

"I just wanted to leave you a flyer," Jerry said. "And ask you to vote for Clifton Saunders next Tuesday."

"That old crook? I thought he died."

"Retired. He's running again."

"I don't want a flyer, thank you." The porch light went off, and the form faded away from the door.

It had been like that much of the day; reaction to Clifton's candidacy ranged from mild annoyance to outright hostility. Jerry couldn't figure it out. As he remembered things, Clifton had been an okay mayor. His Virginia accent had always struck Jerry as a bit out of place in northern New Hampshire, but what did that have to do with being mayor? Jerry remembered the Armed Services Day and Fourth of July parades he'd seen as a child when Clifton rode in the lead convertible as Grand Marshall, his hair so white it seemed almost like a halo, and his eyes discernibly sky blue even at a distance as he stood in the back of the car waving, smiling, and yet somehow solemn.

Even after Clifton had retired and Jerry and Willa grew up, married, and bought a small house two doors up from Clifton's place, Clifton had remained dignified and vaguely ceremonial in Jerry's eyes. Clifton was stocky now. The flesh hung loosely on his face, and his eyelids puffed like small awnings over his eyes.

Watching Clifton rake his leaves or put up his Christmas decorations always made Jerry feel that he was witnessing the acts of an historically significant figure—someone who'd missed becoming governor by fewer than a thousand votes.

And Jerry sensed that there was something to be learned about life from the grace with which Clifton performed the mundane tasks of shoveling his sidewalk in the winter, or washing his old gray Lincoln each spring. The fact that Clifton left his Christmas decorations up until Easter also struck Jerry as a deliberate and meaningful act, not just an eccentricity, as he heard his neighbors say with their smug glances as they walked by Clifton's place.

Jerry shoved his hands into his pockets with the cold campaign flyers. He watched the street for another moment then decided to go home. It was the first day he'd worked with any diligence at putting out flyers, and he was ashamed of himself for having spent the past two months of Saturdays and Sundays watching TV and shooting pool with his friend Chip instead of knocking on doors for Clifton. He was, after all, Clifton's campaign manager. Or so he liked to think.

Clifton had introduced himself one September afternoon when Jerry was giving his small lawn a final summer mowing.

"I used to be mayor of Berlin," Clifton said, rearing back slightly, his blue eyes narrowing with deliberation and importance. "I'm coming out of retirement to run again."

"Yessir. I read about that in the paper."

"There's going to be a meeting at my house tonight. My Inner Sanctum, so to speak. You're welcome to join us, if you'd like."

That evening, Clifton wore a three-piece suit when he answered the door. Newspapers from all over the state were scattered around the living room tables and floor.

"You're the first one here," Clifton said, beaming with charm and solicitous grace. He began to gather up the newspapers, as if he'd forgotten he had company coming.

"Sorry about the mess," he said. "I try to keep up on what's going on around the state. Especially what those rascals in Concord are up to."

On the coffee table in front of the couch were plastic wine glasses—Jerry counted twenty of them. A plate of diced cheese, a toothpick jabbed with upright precision into each tiny cube, sat next to a basket of crackers. Bottles of champagne stuck up from six plastic pails full of ice by the coffee table. Even in the dim light of his living room, Clifton's eyes shone brightly, and the floor lamp behind him made his immaculately combed white hair glow with a greenish fire.

As they waited for more campaigners to arrive, Clifton chatted about how he'd come north from Virginia—Tidewater Country, he called it—when he was a young man, taken a job in the paper mill, eventually opened a grocery store then a second and a third, learned to talk French, as most of the locals did back then, and then made a run for the mayor's office.

"I'm the only one who could get the French vote with an English name," he said, a small grin darting toward the prim corners of his mouth. "I brought some integrity to the office. And accountability to the voters." The grin grew. "I was a worker. Made the job a full-time occupation. In my two terms, we built parks, repaved streets, renovated the gym at the high school. You name it. These folks kinda thought an old Southern boy would just lay back and let events take their own course. But I *made* things happen. I was used to hard work, crabbing, growing potatoes on my daddy's potato farm up on the Eastern Shore. We grew some fine potatoes. Much better than they grow over in Maine.

"Plus, I had the discipline that comes from military training. Air Force. I was stationed down in Portsmouth for the better part of four years, and when my hitch was up, I decided to just stay right here in New Hampshire." Clifton smiled a little sadly. "I met my dearly departed Sarah, who was from here. My fate was sealed." But in a moment his smile recaptured its shine. "Now Sarah, the way we met was kind of interesting. . . ."

Clifton told Jerry his stories for two hours as they waited for the others, but no one else arrived. Clifton looked out the front window a hundred times, and his shoulders seemed to sag a little more each time he returned to the couch.

"Nobody ever worked harder than I did as mayor," he said, his eyes beginning to look tired and pinched. "I guess people just forget."

Jerry emptied a bottle of champagne into his glass and resolved to do whatever it took to help Clifton win the election. This was possibly a great man—a man of drive and conviction. Someone willing to speak up for what he believed in, although Jerry wasn't exactly sure what that might be. As he walked home to Willa, Jerry felt like a man who had been entrusted with an important task. Lying in bed, charged with excitement, he recalled a few televised moments from his non-political past: Kennedy urging people to ask what they could do for their country; Reagan talking about morning in America. Jerry found it amusing that he was suddenly inspired by words that had previously struck him as drab and irrelevant when he thought about them at all.

Willa awoke and asked him what he was doing. Unable to

sleep Jerry sat at the window looking down toward Clifton's house.

"Just thinking."

"About what?"

"Politics. I might just learn what I can from Mayor Saunders and run for some kind of office myself."

Willa rolled over in the bed, away from Jerry. "Please don't."

But Jerry's September campaign ardor was soon replaced by World Series fever, and then by football mental illness. The two thousand campaign flyers Clifton had given Jerry to distribute sat on a shelf in Jerry's pantry, reminding him the first few mornings as he poured his Wheaties into a bowl that a campaign was waiting to be waged. And every night, Clifton telephoned to talk campaign strategy. Jerry would either watch TV or nod off as Clifton held forth.

"What do you think of that approach?" Clifton would ask.

"I think it's great, Mayor."

"Good. Good. That's what we'll do then. So, how many flyers did you put out last weekend?"

It was the moment of the recurring lie. "Oh, three, four hundred . . . maybe more."

"Wonderful. Jerry, I'm just terribly pleased to have a loyal, insightful, hard-working man like you running my campaign."

"It's my pleasure, Mayor."

At the paper mill, where he was an inventory supervisor, Jerry had mentioned that he was working in Clifton's campaign. Most of his coworkers, the older ones anyway, would smirk and shake their heads.

"That crazy old bat? What's he wanna be mayor for at his age?" Jerry would defend Clifton as a very dignified, classy man who had the best manners of anyone he'd ever known.

"He was crazy as hell when he was mayor," someone would inevitably say. "He always had some kind of shit going with somebody. Aldermen, police chief, some school superintendent. Always stirring up the pot."

After hanging up from his nightly conversations with Clifton, Jerry would pace and feel guilty, promise himself that next weekend he'd swing into action and start campaigning in earnest. But it wasn't until the weekend just before the election that Jerry, whose procrastination had rendered him immobile, marshaled himself into action.

*****

When Jerry got home that night from his first campaign blitz, Willa was peeling apples. She hardly glanced up at him. When Jerry felt guilty about things, his lax performance as a campaign worker, for instance, he most envied her tidy approach to life: get your chores done, get your play done (she did two or three cross-word puzzles a night), and get a good night's sleep so you'll be alert at work in the morning. She was a secretary for the school system. She had short, brown hair that curled under her ears and eyes that seemed to flash for an instant when she looked at some-thing or someone. They began dating at their junior prom, seven years earlier, and had been married for almost five years. She had, in theory at least, talked Jerry into having a child, although the pregnancy, like the political campaign, hadn't happened yet.

"Thank God. The Inner Sanctum has arrived," she said. "You'd better go down to Clifton's. He's been up here twice and called about ten times."

"I'll get some supper and go see him." As Jerry looked at the stove to see what Willa had made, the phone rang. "Well . . . maybe I'll go see him before supper after all."

Jerry didn't bother to put on his coat. The smell of the paper mill seemed stronger as he hurried down the street to Clifton's. The door opened before Jerry had a chance to knock. Clifton wore an old burgundy satin robe with holes in the sleeves, his hair was disheveled, and his eyes snapped with rage.

"How many people did you see today?"

Jerry felt good to report truthfully, for a change. "Two hun-dred and eighty or so. . . . Maybe more."

Clifton snatched a letter from his bathrobe pocket and thrust it toward Jerry. "Did any of them mention this?"

Jerry glanced at the letter. With Clifton pacing and ranting, it took Jerry a minute to figure out what the letter said. Clifton snatched it back and pointed to the header.

"Committee of Concerned Taxpayers. I called that number and it's a damned gas station in Nashua. Cloutier is sending out lies from a *gas station*. We'll nail him for mail fraud. *And* libel."

"It's just garbage, Mayor. Don't pay any attention."

"I want you to call Cloutier right now and let him know that we're onto him. I'll listen in while you're talking. I can tell from his voice whether he's the one behind it."

"*Call* him, Mayor? Are you sure?"

"Yes, I'm sure." Clifton started walking toward the kitchen, but Jerry stayed in the dark living room. Clifton motioned to him to follow. "I want to show you something."

Jerry was relieved when Clifton walked past the telephone and opened the door onto his back porch. Dozens of CLOUTIER FOR MAYOR posters lay on their sides against the screen walls.

"Look at those. Every one of them was nailed to a live tree.

That's against the law. I go out at night and pull them down. I'd appreciate it if you'd do the same, anytime you're out driving late at night."

"But . . . it's only three days until the election."

Clifton ignored him. "I'll put them up for insulation this winter. Keep the snow and ice off this porch."

"Good idea, Mayor."

"Come on back inside. I want you to tell Cloutier you're part of a committee to protect the trees from people who nail posters on them. That will put him on the defensive. Then you can ask him point-blank if he's the one who's been putting out the letter saying I stole from the city retirement fund. Remind him that he *bought* his way in to that fund. I said at the time that it was illegal, and I stand by that statement."

"Wait a minute, Mayor . . . let's talk about this."

But Clifton was already dialing the number, his mouth in a tight, flat line. As soon as it began to ring at the other end, Clifton rammed the phone toward Jerry.

"Hello?"

"Eh, hello. Councilman Cloutier?"

"Right here. Who's this, please?"

"Mr. Cloutier, I'm . . . well, I'm calling on behalf of a local organization . . . that . . ."

"I'm glad to hear from your organization."

"Well, eh . . . you might not be so glad, Councilman. I mean, I'm calling to register a complaint."

Cloutier's voice became reserved. "What organization did you say you're with?"

"I'm calling on behalf . . . of the . . . The Friends of the Trees, Sir. We want to complain about the way you nail campaign posters to live trees."

Cloutier cleared his throat. "Oh. Yes. Some of my campaign workers get a bit enthusiastic. Want to put posters everywhere."

Jerry felt a sharp nudge. Clifton was scribbling on a pad of paper, which he held up for Jerry to read. In large letters was written, *ask him about that damn letter from the Committee of Concerned Voters!* Jerry nodded.

". . . They just nail signs to everything. Live trees, dead ones, telephone poles; you name it. I go out sometimes after dark and pull down the ones that are nailed to *live* trees. I should probably be in your club, ha ha."

Jerry wanted to ask him if he was planning to insulate his porch. He immediately disliked Councilman Cloutier, whom he'd never met. Clifton nudged Jerry again; he'd underlined the words on the message. Jerry nodded while Cloutier droned on.

". . . Course I've told them a hundred times not to nail things to trees. They'll clean everything up after the election and all the trees will be just fine."

"Maybe not, Mr. Cloutier. I've seen maples bleed when nails were put in them."

"That's sap, Young Fella. That's what maples do."

Clifton shook the pad frantically. A new message was scrawled there, and it took Jerry several moments to decipher it. Cloutier's voice crept back into the pause.

"I'd be happy to visit your club and apologize. I try to get to at least one meeting of all the local . . ."

"We're a *national* organization," Jerry said, his voice rising. "Not just local."

"Well . . . whatever," Cloutier said. "I'm very big on the environmental movement myself. Unlike my opponent, who's not from around here. I believe the voters will give him a bowl of grits and send him back where he belongs. Ha ha."

There was a new message scrawled on Clifton's pad: *Ask him about his bill to double the pensions of aldermen!*

"Anyway, I appreciate your call. Tell all your members I'd appreciate their votes for mayor of this great little city."

Jerry's indignation was instant and genuine. "We're not voting for anyone who nails posters to trees."

Cloutier laughed. "Well, I guess you won't be voting, then. Everybody from mayor down to dogcatcher has signs nailed to trees."

"Not Mayor Saunders."

Clifton looked up sharply at the mention of his name.

Cloutier laughed again. "Well, I beg to differ. I've seen Clifton's posters on trees. He'd nail a sign to a stray dog if it'd stand still long enough. I'm surprised the animal rights people haven't put him away."

Clifton, growing more frantic, shook his writing pad at Jerry and stomped his foot. His quivering finger pointed to a new message: *Ask him about giving that park maintenance contract to his brother!*

Jerry felt a pressure in the back of his neck as the blood pounded in his head. "I'm sorry, Mr. Cloutier, but you're wrong." Jerry turned away, but Clifton immediately moved back in front of him and waved his pad an inch in front of Jerry's face.

Cloutier's voice brightened to a jeer when he spoke again. "I didn't get your name, but all of a sudden I have this funny feeling that you're calling from Clifton's house. Am I right? Clifton put you up to this. . . ."

Clifton grabbed Jerry's shirt collar and rammed the writing pad into his face. Jerry struggled to get away, but Clifton's grip was strong. Cloutier broke into full laughter now.

"You tell Clifton I'm taping this whole conversation and that I plan to turn the tape over to the newspaper. And tell that old bastard he's losing his mind if all he has to do on a Saturday night is make prank calls to his neighbors."

Clifton wrenched the phone away and wheezed into it like a bull who had been only grazed by the first sword. "Cloutier," he bellowed, "You miserable pile of snake shit . . . I'll kill you for spreading lies about me." Clifton's hair was more and more disheveled, and he grasped it in bunches as he screamed into the telephone. "I mean, I'll come over there with an axe and take your balls off and serve them to the fucking pigeons!"

Jerry edged toward the living room and waited there in the dark a few more minutes.

"You're the wormiest piece of scum that ever tried to lick the shit off a dead dog!"

When Clifton's voice began to hurt his ears, Jerry slipped outside, closing the door quietly behind him. Clifton's voice still roared, and Jerry looked around, wondering if anyone else could hear the ruckus.

He told Willa what had happened, and she shook her head. "Do you think he'd actually kill Cloutier?"

Jerry didn't know how to answer. He'd never seen a person as angry as Clifton Saunders was at that moment with Paul Cloutier.

Within minutes, two police cars coasted down the street and stopped in front of Clifton's. They parked, turned their lights off, and disappeared inside Clifton's house. Jerry and Willa watched from their porch as the policemen escorted Clifton, who had changed into a suit, to the police car. Clifton noticed Jerry and waved to him.

"I'm fine. You don't need to do anything." In a lowered voice, Clifton said to the cops, "that's my campaign manager."

Shortly after that, when Jerry and Willa went to bed, Jerry lay awake a long time watching the headlights of the few cars that passed outside stagger faintly across the wall. When he realized that Willa was awake, he touched her shoulder.

"Yes?"

"Do you think I'm loyal and hard-working?" he asked.

"What kind of a question is that?"

He hesitated. "A bad one I guess."

"You're loyal enough."

"Loyal enough for what?"

"I don't know," she said. "Just loyal enough. Why? Are you about to confess that you've been *dis*loyal?"

"No. It's just that Clifton thinks I'm loyal and hard-working. And everybody in town seems to think Clifton's crazy."

She studied him a moment in the light from the street lamp then touched his face. He knew it was the dangerous time of the month, according to the calendar, which he always kept careful track of, but he could not resist her when she touched him like that. Her eyes had that glow he'd loved for so long.

She put her arms around his neck. "Come here," she whispered.

*****

The next day, Sunday, Jerry started out early. Few doors opened to his knock. Everyone was at church, he guessed. He left flyers tucked in beside doorknobs, then drove to the church parking lots and left flyers on car windshields, too.

More people were home in the afternoon, and Jerry thought he detected amusement as he went from door to door making his pitch. At one house, Jerry could hear a radio in the background. It was the local talk radio station, and Clifton was on the air, calling from the jail, where he'd been charged with making threatening phone calls. He remained there when he refused to pay bail.

As he put out flyers, Jerry noticed that every radio in the city seemed to be tuned in to the Saunders-Cloutier war story. He heard a familiar line from Cloutier: "The voters of this city ought to give Clifton Saunders a bowl of grits and send him back where he came from. He never belonged here anyway."

On Monday Jerry called his boss to take a vacation day, then went out to campaign. Most people were at work, but Jerry left fliers anyway, finally emptying the heavy carton and going home.

Willa had seen no sign of Clifton, whose car was still in his driveway. Jerry wondered if he should go down to the jail and try to bail him out, but he decided that would only anger Clifton, who was obviously getting some mileage out of the jailing.

On Tuesday Jerry took yet another vacation day. He visited some of the polling places, as he knew Clifton would have, but the situation struck him as depressing. Clifton didn't come home election night, either, and Jerry went to bed before the late returns came on TV, not wanting to know how badly Clifton had been beaten.

But at seven o'clock the next morning, there was a loud banging on the porch, and the doorbell blasted in three short rings at a time. Jerry stood at the door, not wanting to open it. Clifton would understandably blame him for the loss, and Jerry would have to admit that it was, indeed, all his fault.

The bell continued to ring, and Jerry gritted his eyes shut for a moment before he opened the door. Clifton, combed and dapper once again, said nothing. He only puffed in an importantly deep breath and held up the newspaper.

"That's great, Mayor. Gosh. I mean . . . congratulations."

Clifton thrust a wrapped bottle toward Jerry. "This is for you. Just a thank you for running a good, old-fashioned, hard-nosed campaign for me." He grinned. "'Course, when it came right down to the nitty-gritty, I didn't exactly shy away."

Jerry could tell by the feel of the package that it was a bottle of champagne, probably left over from the first time he visited Clifton's place.

"When the going gets tough," Clifton continued, "the tough raise holy hell."

"Amen, Mayor. . . ."

Clifton started back to his own house, first at a trot but slowing after a few steps to a reflective walk. He waved without looking back. "See you in four years. Maybe sooner. Mayors sometimes have jobs for people who know how to get things done."

He stopped at a leafless young maple and touched a twig, as if he was the one who'd made it, then continued steadily on, where he disappeared inside his house

HOW THE HOG ATE THE CABBAGE

For Sarah Orne Jewett

Stover Stackhouse stood behind a tree and watched his son Herbert, who sat astraddle the ridge pole of the barn, high up, just in back of the weathervane. The November sun had warmed the season's first snow to a slow melt, and half of the snow that had accumulated on the roof had already seeped away.

Stover knew exactly what Herbert could see from there—a small field, a stretch of pines, and a few sun-glistened spots of the brook that eventually found its way to the lake. Most of all, Herbert could see Lakeside Lodge, a place where elderly people, mostly from Massachusetts, came to stay in the summer. Stover noticed that his son's head seldom moved, and that his stare was fixed in the direction of the lodge.

It was owned by a man from outside Boston named Goldstein— Moldy Goldy, as the people in Waterford called him. He was now in his seventies, old enough to be hard of hearing and soft of mind, Stover had surmised many years ago. Although Mr. Goldstein was said to be rich, he wore old overalls and moth-holed flannel shirts all summer as he puttered around his lodge, nailing a loose fence slat back into place, or gathering up the tennis balls that his guests had slapped out of the decrepit clay courts and not bothered to retrieve.

Moldy Goldy gave Stover work each summer doing odd jobs. Stover was changing out a broken sink pipe one afternoon when Mr. Goldstein offered to sell Stover the lodge and hold the note himself. Stover, who owned a small hardware and cattle feed store uptown and never felt that the summer trade was reliable enough to depend on, declined the offer.

But Herb, who had just turned fifteen, piped up and said by God he'd like to buy it. He was a stocky, muscular kid who had the air of someone who had never had to pass through childhood and had, instead, been born in overalls directly into the working world.

When both Stover and Mr. Goldstein continued to stare at him, Goldstein with an amused smile and Stover with regret that Herb had heard Goldstein's offer, Herb piped up again.

"Why the hell not? What's that mean, you hold the note?"

Stover Stackhouse and Sam Goldstein glanced at each other, Goldstein with a smirk in his eyes, Stover with his old question: *how could a sedate, stable man such as himself sire the likes of a tornado like Herbert?*

*****

Now, ordinarily it'd take three, four hours to cut one cord of wood doing it the regular way. Me and Buddy'd get on either side of a two-man buck saw and hack like hell till the sweat was pourin' off. By the time we'd get through four or five logs Buddy'd have to take a break. I never was much of a sweater myself, so I'd just set in the shade while Buddy did his moanin' and groanin' about how hot it was. We'd be doing this in July, August so's we could get a jump on the others out peddlin' fire wood in September. We'd spend the whole damned day killing ourselves for ten dollars each.

When we got our hands on that first chain saw, we thought we was just about ready to show everybody in Waterford, Bridgton and Harrison how the hog ate the cabbage. That was an expression we picked up from old Hod Miller, Buddy's stepfather. He was from Alabama and was always coming out with stuff we couldn't hardly figure out, but we knew it had to have some deep meaning.

Old Hod Miller was a good one to help out. He had a beat-up Ford flatbed he'd rent us at two dollars a week to haul the pulp that the logging crews left out in the woods for Buddy and me. We'd cut it for firewood and get six dollars a cord for pine and fir, eight dollars a cord for ash and birch and oak and maple. Buddy and me worked with the loggers on the weekend. The men all said we was good sawyers, especially for being so young. We was in high school, but we wanted to quit and work full time.

You see, we'd had a little taste of making money and that's what we wanted to do. I had about four, five businesses on the side. For one thing, I shoveled snow up in town in the winter. In the summer, I had a little concession with the folks in the cabins down on the lake just below our house. My old man had over a thousand hens. I figured he wouldn't miss a few if I sold fryers to the summer people, but I was wrong. The old man could look at a coop of hens and tell you in a glance how many there was, give or take one or two. 'Long about August, he laid a trap and caught me. I was coming out of the barn cellar with eight hens all picked nice and clean, and four, five dozen eggs. I cut into the woods toward the lake, and there he was, about fifty yards down the path, leaning against a tree.

"Fella with a chicken business oughta have his own chickens," he said.

He made me give him back the money I'd made on *his* chick-

ens, forty or fifty dollars, and I thought that was that. But the
next thing I knew, he took and bought me a hundred hens of my
own. So I was making about five dollars a week off'n them hens,
plus maybe ten a week cutting trees for the loggers, and another
ten, twelve sawing pulp with Buddy. What we didn't sell for firewood, we'd sell to the paper company for two dollars a load.

Now that don't sound like much, but it was good money for
a kid in nineteen and fifty. A quart of milk was about twenty
cents then, and a pack of smokes was about the same. Then one
day everything changed. One of the Ridlon brothers showed up
in the woods on a Sat'dy morning and he's got a new toy. It was
this funny looking thing, kind of a big steel ball with this long
paddle thing sticking out.

"What in hell is that?"

"Chainsaw," Kenny Ridlon says.

Kenny filled the thing with gas, then started yanking on this
cord. The thing started up like a motorcycle without no muffler.
Old Kenny takes the thing over to a tree and starts in. That saw
gnawed away like a big dog growling over a bone. In about thirty
seconds, down comes the tree—a good sized one, too. Thirteen,
fourteen inches. I knew from the way Buddy was smiling at that
chain saw that we was going to have to have one. It didn't make
no difference in the woods; we was going to make eighty-five cents
an hour no matter how many trees we cut down. But cutting firewood was going to be different. I moved over a little closer to
Buddy and hollered in his ear.

"Probably cut a cord of pulp in half an hour."

He nodded.

"Probably cut fifteen cords on a weekend."

Buddy nodded again. "One of us cutting, one stacking."

You'd a thought with all the money I was making, I could a
come up with three hundred for a chain saw like I was just buying
a pack of smokes, but I was bad about taking out from what I'd
been putting away. I did have one special purpose in mind I was
putting away for, and that part was untouchable. I even had it in
the bank, just to keep it away from me.

"I ain't got it today, but I'll have it a week from now. I'll sure
as hell have it before school starts."

There warn't nothin I hated quite like school. I'd try to fake
sick two or three times a month, or else I'd just skip. The old
man'd give me a talking to, I'd go to school every day for a week,
then I'd try to fake sick again. School was about to start up, so I
went to the old man. He was in the garden picking squash.

"Why don't you lend me a hundred and fifty?" I says.

"What for?"

"It's a secret."

"Nope."

"Okay. How's this, if you'll lend me that hundred and fifty, I'll consider going back to school next month."

"You will, huh? That's mighty generous of you."

"Pa, I hate school and you know it."

"Life's tough everywhere."

"Okay, how's this? I'll pay you back before school starts, plus I'll go back to school this fall."

"Son, how's this? Pass everything, graduate next June, and I'll *give* you a hundred and fifty."

I figured by then everybody in Bridgton would have a chain saw, and Buddy 'n' me would be pretty much shut out of the firewood business.

"Look, Pa . . . I know a way I can make a pile of dough."

"Honest or dishonest?"

I figured he was remembering the chicken episode. "Honest. Me and Buddy want to buy a chain saw."

"What in hell is a chain saw?"

I talked him into going uptown to Potter's Hardware. I figured once he saw a chain saw with his own eyes, he'd be so impressed he'd buy me one on the spot. But the old man was a hard sell.

"Damned thing'd break down and then where would you be? Three hundred dollars down the drain. I think you'd best go back to school next month and forget about chain saws."

That next week I asked everybody I knew to lend me the money. Word got out to the old man, and he was furious.

"What are you, a beggar?"

"No. I just want a chain saw."

"All right. I'll lend you the money. But if you miss a single day of school this year, the chain saw goes back to Potter's, and your ass goes in the army. I heard they could use a few like you over in Korea!"

*****

Stover had often thought that if Herbert studied as hard as he worked and day-dreamed, the boy would have been one of the top students in the state of Maine. It had been nearly three years since Herbert got it in his mind that he was going to buy Lakeside Lodge and began to spend hours at a time up on the barn roof staring out over the trees, owning the place already. From the barn roof, Stover knew, Herbert could see only a dormer and part of the lodge's porch, even with the trees mostly bare, now that it was fall. But Stover knew how his son's mind worked. Herbert was seeing through that roof into the large, paneled rec room with its pool table and ping-pong tables, into the dining room with its single, long table that sat forty-two people. Or into the old wooden castle's twenty-six bedrooms, where the mattresses had been stripped to air for the winter.

By the time he was ten Herbert had figured out ways to get inside the building when it was empty—when all the guests had gone back to Waltham or Hingham or Worcester, and Mr. Goldstein had gone home to Brookline for the winter. Or to Florida, where he had a house-boat big enough to live on. During the winter, Herbert would light a few logs in the massive stone fireplace, then sit in a rocking chair by the window watching the still eyes of the mounted moose heads, or looking out over the white lake and the whiteness of the hills on the other side. Stover knew what Herbert was up to; he'd followed him and stayed back to observe. Besides, Stover could smell the wood fire from his place—and its ghost all over Herbert's clothes whenever he returned from one of his meditations and would be in his best moods.

Stover never worried that Herbert would burn the place down, only that the boy was obsessed, and Stover considered even the healthi-est obsession dangerous.

*****

I was right about how fast chain saws would catch on. By the time me and Buddy went up to Potter's to buy ours, they'd already sold about six of them. But we went to work cutting fire-wood, and in two days we'd gone and cut damn near ten cords. We borrowed Hod Miller's flatbed to deliver it all, and for about two weeks, we had more business than we could keep up with. I was making around a hundred a week. Pa was right about one thing—the chain saw broke down every few days, but me and Buddy figured out how to fix it ourselves. When school started we kept working weekends, but school was a torture, knowing we could make a hundred a week working everyday. I'd look across the room—the teachers hadn't let us sit side one another since about third grade—in Algebra class, Buddy'd look right back, and either me or him would hold a saw in the air and yank the cord. The other one would nod and pull his own cord.

When I say we worked weekends, I mean we started cutting when we got out of school on Friday afternoon, and we cut until it got too dark to see. Then we'd be at it by six in the morning and work a good twelve, thirteen hours. Pa made me go to church with him Sunday mornings, but I was out of my monkey suit and back in the woods by noon. I was so tired, I'd generally go to bed right after supper. All I could think about was my chain saw, and most nights I'd dream about it. That old thing just buzzed and spit and hacked and tore through the logs like some kind of a wild animal. Me and Buddy took turns taking the thing home with us. During my turns I always kept it in the bedroom with me. I'd set it on this little table I had over by the window so it would get lit up by the moon.

Homework? By the end of September, I was failing every course except physical education. The teachers sent Pa a notice. He stopped me out in the barn on Saturday morning.

"Give me the chain saw."

"But I been goin' to school everyday . . . damn it"

He locked the chain saw in the trunk of his car. I had to stay home and study the whole weekend. Buddy came by to pick me up when the old man told him the story. Buddy took the saw and went out to cut by himself. The firewood season was too short for me to be wasting a weekend studying. The competition to sell firewood that year was fierce because of all the new chainsaws around. I was checking in at Potter's every few days to find out how many more they'd sold. It's tough to study biology when you got that much on your mind.

During the next week I flunked a history test and a English test. Pa had the teachers notify him directly whenever I got a new grade in anything. So Friday rolls around and there I am cooped up again with the books. Potter's was selling two or three chain saws a week. I had to put a stop to that, so I put up my summer savings as a down payment on the three they had in stock so's no one else could buy them. Now I owed for three chain saws I didn't need. It came to almost a thousand dollars. When I tried to put up a down payment on two more saws, I guess Mr. Potter rang up the old man. When he got home from work that night, Pa came into my room. I heard him coming and grabbed a book.

"Sam Potter says he ain't turning down good money from people just 'cause you don't want folks buying chain saws."

"I'm just . . ."

"You need to forget that chain saw and buckle down on the books. No more wood cutting until you start passing."

Me and Buddy talked it over next Monday. I don't know how he was passing when I was flunking. I guess he could just concentrate better. Think about more than just one thing at a time.

We'd cut wood late at night, I told him. I'd sneak out around eleven, we'd work until four or five, then we'd get back home before anyone in the house woke up. We did that for three nights, working by the headlights on Hod Miller's flatbed. Then I couldn't handle it any more. Everybody for sixty miles around seemed to want wood, and it was painful to turn them down. We cut wood four nights in a row and delivered it after school—thirteen cords in one week—until the rain came, which was a good thing because I was about ready to drop.

I didn't even try to fake sick; I just finally had to go to bed and stay there for a couple of days. The old man left me alone, and I lay abed, listening to the rain and thinking about all my money, which I spend as fast as I made. I didn't have a single chain saw dream.

But on Monday morning after that, Pa come into my room before the sun was even up and ordered me to get dressed. We got in the car together, and I wasn't the least bit surprised when he drove right through town and brought me to Portland to the army recruiting center. I knew he figured he had to go through with sticking me in the army. That was what he'd threatened to do, and Pa was a man of his word.

*****

It was six, already dark, and Stover flipped on the yard light as he came out of the house. Herbert, jacketless, still sat on the barn roof, only a silhouette now. Stover figured he was, in his own odd way, saying his good-byes to home. The temperature had taken a sharp drop, freezing the wetness from the melted snow on the roof into a shiny coat that glistened in the yard light.

"Better come down. Before you catch pneumonia."

Herbert neither answered nor stirred. Stover watched a few minutes, then went back inside. But something about the way Herbert seemed frozen in place up there in the dark sent Stover back outside again.

"You all right?" Stover's breathing came a little faster as he studied the situation. The barn and house were twin buildings connected by a shed whose sharp roofline ran perpendicular to the house and barn. The ladder leaned against the shed.

Herbert shifted a little, and a small, choked-back curse escaped from him as he started to slip. He grabbed the metal rod of the weathervane, but when he tried to let go, his fingers stuck.

"Shit," Herbert mumbled. "Stuck."

"Just hold 'er steady, Son. We'll figure something out."

Back inside, Stover called the fire department, but it was only a volunteer department, and whoever answered the phone, a voice Stover did not recognize, said it would be at least thirty minutes before they could get anyone down there. Stover ran back outside.

"Don't pull," he hollered up at Herbert. "You'll just tear your skin off."

*****

I figured flunking the army would be about as easy as flunking English. Pa parked about a half a block away from the recruiting office and pointed. I got out of the car, feeling pretty good about things, considering. The sergeant that interviewed me had a huge jaw that jutted out like a bulldozer plow and eyes that were small and mean. He asked me all these questions about my health. I told him I was a little deaf, borderline blind, afraid of the dark and real jumpy in broad daylight. He had me fill out this questionnaire, and when I saw some of the questions I wanted to laugh. When he asked me if I ever wet the bed accidentally, I told him no, I did it on purpose. He looked at me kind of alarmed. Then he asked me if I liked girls. I told him I wasn't sure yet.

"But I love to kill," I told him.

His eyes got big. "Oh yeah? Like what?"

"Once when I was a little kid, I killed a hen with a screwdriver. It pecked me." The sergeant sat back in his chair and stared at me. I guess he was waiting for me to look away, but I didn't.

"We'll let you know," he said.

Pa and me headed back to Bridgton. Pa was real quiet, like we wasn't going to be seeing much of each other for a long time. I played along with him. I already had a plan worked out.

"Well, I guess I'll just cut wood till they call me up."

"You'll stay in school. Be awhile before they call you up."

"But Pa . . . I could cut a lot of wood and make a good stash before I go off. Leave you a little something in case I get killed over there. I know damn well you ain't got much of Ma's insurance money left."

"I don't need more insurance money. Or any other kind, Son. You're going back to school tomorrow, and you're staying there until they call you up for basic."

I could tell by the way his voice shook that I wouldn't be able to talk him out of it. But, like I said, I had a plan. I'd start cutting wood and missing school. Then the army would notify me I flunked their interview. I'd a missed so much school at that point I'd have to wait until next year to finish up. And by then, I figured I'd have so much money that Mr. Truman himself couldn't tell me what to do.

Next morning I skipped. I cut wood all day. When I got home that night, Pa didn't say a word, even though I could tell he knew I'd skipped. Morning after that, I tried to cut some wood, but the loggers I was following hadn't left enough brush for a crippled beaver. All day long I kept thinking of the five chain saws I owed for and couldn't use. I was the better part of two thousand in debt and didn't know where I could make ten dollars. The summer people were long gone, so the chicken business was dried up. It was already November, so anybody that wanted fire wood had it laid in already. And he paper mill wasn't buying pulp for two months. Mr. Potter was calling me twice a week to come to pick up my saws—if I had the money—or he'd hafta sell them. He reminded me that the down payments was all non-refundable.

I started acting a little crazy. I still kept the chain saw up in my room, and sometimes I even talked to it. And then it rained for a week, soaking every stick of wood I'd cut. Then it froze, just to keep it all good and wet. And then the first storm of the year hit. It snowed eighteen inches. To top things off, I let the oil get so low in Hod Miller's flatbed that I threw a rod. I already owed him twenty-two dollars in rent for the thing. Now I owed him a engine, too.

So, when the army wrote and said they wanted me to come in for a physical, I jumped on it. I figured they must have known I was faking crazy when I came in that first time. If anybody asked me about being blind, deaf, or a little strange, I was planning to tell them I got over it. But nobody asked.

It took almost two weeks to hear that I'd passed my physical, then another three weeks before I was supposed to ship out to basic. I worked out my debts with old Sam Potter up at the hardware store. When I told him I was going in the army, he let me off the hook. So did Hod Miller. He just happened to have another engine right there in his back yard.

*****

Stover's feet slipped on the icy rungs of the wooden ladder as he climbed to the eave of the woodshed roof. He shined a flashlight up toward Herbert and saw that the boy was shivering all over as he clung to the weathervane.

"I got help coming, Son. Just hold on. I'm gonna try to throw this blanket over you."

"I'm too damned cold for a blanket to make much difference."

Stover noticed the anger in Herbert's voice and took hope in the heat that such anger might generate. He watched his own breath rise into the beam of the flashlight, which he kept trained on Herbert.

"Just keep talking to me," Stover said.

"I ain't got all that much to say."

"Say it anyway. . . ."

"Well, for openers, I'm goddamn mad that we let Moldy Goldy sell that place right out from in under us. I had the money for a down payment. Busted my ass for three years for nothing!"

Ordinarily, Stover would have told Herbert to watch his language. But tonight, Stover let him swear all he wanted. He had a right to.

"They're gonna turn it into a friggin' campground. And the lodge is going to be a rec hall. They'll wreck it, all right. No damn doubt about it."

*****

It was my old man who was the most torn up about me going off in the army. It didn't make a hell of a lot of difference to me, especially with the lodge gone. He kept saying he'd been too hard on me and shouldn't have got so upset when I was skipping school. Like he finally admitted, I was just trying to make some money. It warn't like I was loafing or getting in trouble. He'd never been in the army himself; he was too young for One, too old for Two. He kept telling me he was proud of me and all that kind of stuff, but that I needed to learn how to manage myself. I never heard him talk so much in one hour.

And then he started to cry. My old man just didn't do that. He told me what had really happened was the recruiting sergeant was a friend of his who used to live there in Bridgton, and that he'd worked it out with him to give me a pretend physical and scare me into studying harder. He never intended for me to actually go off to war. But we got there on a day when his friend was off sick. The sergeant who was filling in—the one with the huge jaw and the little tiny eyes—he had no idea what my old man was sitting out in the car expecting him to do.

*****

The town fire truck arrived in a little less than thirty minutes, but by the time it got there, Hod Miller had stopped by to show Herbert that he had the flatbed engine fixed so Herbert wouldn't feel bad on his last night home. Hod Miller had a rope, which he tossed over the barn roof just in front of Herbert, secured both ends, and climbed it up to the ridgepole, where he warmed Herbert's hands enough to get them unstuck from the weathervane. He made Herbert put on his jacket, but Herbert knew he'd never be able to hold onto the rope to lower himself to the ground. So they waited there together until the fire truck came.

The people on the fire truck put an extension ladder up the roof, and Herbert, shivering and barely able to hang on with his frostbitten hands, finally made it to the ground. They sat him on the front bumper of the fire engine and wrapped him in blankets. Stover made him some hot chocolate, as much so that Herbert could hold the warm cup in his hands as actually drink it. After a few sips, Herbert was ready to go inside. The firemen got in their truck and left.

Stover and Hod Miller sat with Herbert the kitchen table.

"I had the money and everything," Herbert said. "Woulda had even more in three years. A fella can put aside a few dollars in the

army."

   "*Maybe some other place will come up by then,*" *Stover said, glancing at Hod Miller. Hod nodded. "They's more than one hog,*" *he said. "And they's always more cabbage.*"

   Herbert said nothing, but Stover easily read the scorn in his silence.

*****

So I did basic at Fort Dix in the lovely state of New Jersey in the coldest damn winter on record, then got assigned to the Corps of Engineers and shipped out to Korea the next summer. Come winter, it got about as cold as Maine, but I was used to that so it didn't bother me none. I never did get shot at directly, although some artillery come close a few times.

   This one time I was out in the woods with a platoon of ROK soldiers—those were the good ones—and we was clearing this area to put a road through for tanks. They picked me to show the Koreans how to use a chain saw. They're all gathered around, and I hollered that I was going to show them how the hog ate the cabbage. The little ROK sergeant that was translating looked at me real strange. I held up the saw, which I hadn't started up yet.

   "This here's the hog . . . them trees are the cabbage."

   He still didn't try to translate it. So I yanked the cord and fired that hog up.

   Them ROK people ran in every direction, and I stood there and laughed. Made me kind of wish I did the same thing first time I saw a chainsaw.

Detecting Metal

for O. Henry

George Stockton didn't want to go to the airport in the first place. He'd always lived around Rumford because he didn't want to hear city noises, like jet planes; and he lived two miles outside the town on a dirt road so he wouldn't even have to hear many cars. But his fourth-cousin, Jenna Simmons, was coming from New Orleans to Maine for a visit, and George's sister Merle had more or less ordered George to come along to Portland to greet Jenna as she stepped off the plane. He and Jenna were about the same age, both in their fifties, but George hadn't seen her since they were in high school, where she used to taunt him privately that they would probably end up together one day. Such a threat used to annoy him, not so much because he believed it but rather that she should even express it to him.

In spite of himself, George could not help but wonder what she looked like now—and what she might think about him. He still had the same thick tangle of hair, mostly gray since his mid-forties, and he wore glasses, but only to read his farming magazines and the *Portland Sunday Telegram*. His lingering image of Jenna was a teenager with long, straight black hair that fell nearly to her knees when she let it loose from the usual pony tail. Her eyebrows were thick and shiny back then, and her eyes flashed and flirted. But her tight, bowed lips always wore a scornful, superior pout that put people off. Everyone agreed that she was very pretty, borderline beautiful. Her only physical flaw, the boys at school had decided, was her glasses. The thick lenses exaggerated the size of her eyes and made her look as if she viewed the world from inside an aquarium. Nonetheless, the boys conceded that from the nose down, she was quite the feat of female architecture, whether she was a pain in the ass most of the time or not.

Jenna had now been a widow for over five years. George had never married. Merle and Fat Stuart, as George thought of her husband, ribbed George that no woman would have him because he was so picky about things. George knew he was picky, and he was proud of it. He had no tolerance for what he considered nonsense, and he was constantly on his guard against it. To him, most of what went on in the city was nonsense. People in the city just plain couldn't take care of themselves. If a pipe burst they called a plumber. If the car didn't start, they called the garage. George felt that people who couldn't fix their own pipes or cars basically shouldn't have the right to own them.

George rode in the back, directly behind Fat Stuart, who drove. George thought Stuart was a terrible driver. He went up and down on the gas peddle, which George considered the mortal sin of driving. He drove too slow, gabbing at Merle, who, like her brother, was a reluctant talker unless she had something worth saying.

George had said nothing since they left Rumford, but Stuart chattered away in the front, going on and on about how when he finished his shower that morning, he found that he'd forgotten to put a towel on the rack, and that it was the first time something like that had ever happened to him. Three days ago, George almost didn't bother to get down from his tractor the morning Stuart came out to tell him Jenna was coming home for a visit. Few people ever left Rumford, Jenna being one of those who did. No one had heard from her in twenty years, until a few months ago when Jenna had written to Merle, and the two began a weekly exchange of letters.

What used to irritate George most about Jenna was the way she put on airs. She was not going to stay in Rumford for *her* whole life. She was going to go to Vienna and become a famous violinist and study under Dr. Freud. George had no more idea who Freud was than who Jenna's other heroes were—Picasso and Pavlov and Proust. Jenna would stop in the middle of a sentence and cover her mouth and giggle as she looked at him. "Oh pardon me . . . Georgie . . . I guess you don't know who Sophocles was, do you?" And George would answer that not only did he *not* know who Sophocles was, he also didn't give a good goddamn. Even in his youth, George had grown convinced there wasn't a thing outside of the state of Maine—and possibly even outside the town of Rumford—that held any interest for him.

People had said back then that he was eighteen going on eighty. The army might have forced him to broaden his perspective, but a minor heart murmur had made George undraftable. It made no difference to him whether he went in the army or not, and when George's father died, it was natural that Mother Stockton should stay there on the farm with George rather than go to live with Merle. Mother Stockton could not tolerate Fat Stuart for more than ten minutes at a time. Thanksgiving and Christmas were grueling events since Merle and Stuart would be at the farm for the entire day. George and his mother often wore rubber earplugs that George had bought at the five-and-dime in town.

Mother Stockton greatly preferred the company of George. For the last fifteen years of her life, she and George seldom spoke more than five words to each other on any given day. What pain she might have suffered was smothered in silence, and when she finally slipped away, it was in her sleep, without complaint.

Alone in the family farmhouse, George became even more withdrawn. As the years passed, he had become increasingly suspicious of the world out there. The latest thing to make him apprehensive was computers. The idea that viruses could travel over electrical wires and telephone lines and infect a household filled him with raw hatred. He read widely about computers, much as a general might study the military tactics of an enemy army. The more he read, the more he realized that there was no defense against computers. When Merle and Stuart bought Mother Stockton a computer to entertain herself, since she couldn't get around very well anymore, George, with rifle in hand, met the delivery truck at the gate and refused to let the computer onto his property. The thought of viruses was far more powerful than the flicker of temptation he'd felt when he read that a computer could play chess. Chess had been George's only passion since he was twelve, but no one would play him anymore, since he'd thrashed everyone in town by the time he was eighteen—and been a less than gracious victor. The victories he'd always savored the most were those won at the expense of Jenna Simmons.

✳✳✳✳✳

George disliked the airport from the moment they entered the parking lot. You had to stop in front of a little gate that went up when you pulled a ticket out of a slot in the wall. The next thing George didn't like about the airport was the doors that opened automatically as they approached. Anyone who couldn't open a door for himself ought not to be out in public. Then there was the lobby; plain overdone, George could see. He grimaced at the huge lighted signs advertising hotels and restaurants. There were gift shops, news stands, snack bars, banners welcoming people to Maine, as if the state needed another body meandering around in a tee shirt and sandals. There was enough room inside the terminal for half the state of Maine, even though the place was nearly empty.

"C'mon," Stuart wheezed, waddling toward the escalator. "Let's head on up to the gate right away in case the plane's early."

George walked behind them. Neither Merle nor Stuart noticed George's hesitation at getting on the escalator. He watched some people on the downward side staring ahead, as if they were somehow transfixed. It seemed faked, theatrical, and that made George think of Jenna again. Once when they were eleven or twelve, Jenna announced that she was going to go to Hollywood to learn acting, then to London, where she would become a famous Shakespearean actress with Sir Laurence Olivier. To the best that George knew, she had never managed to become anything fancier than a librarian at some college in New Orleans. He tried to imagine her as a librarian, but he could only picture that long, straight hair, perhaps gray by now but in no way dignified enough to make her look like any librarian he'd ever seen.

George had forgotten to pay attention to the escalator and he stumbled getting off. Ahead was a small doorframe with two uniformed men watching them approach.

"George! No, George, you can't go that way," Stuart croaked in a panic. "You haffta go through this here gate."

George stopped. A security guard motioned him to come back and walk through the makeshift doorframe.

"This way, George," Stuart directed. "Through there." Stuart handed his car keys and some loose change to the guards. Merle handed them her purse.

George backed up. Merle and Stuart had walked through the frame and now waited for him. George took one long stride to get through, and a buzzer sounded.

"Wait," the guard said. "You got to come on back."

George looked at the guard, a young guy with a thin mustache, a starched, light blue uniform shirt, and what George thought seemed like a high opinion of himself.

"C'mon back," the guard said again.

George went back through the gate and the buzzer sounded again. "What in hell is that?" he demanded.

"Metal detector. Security." The guard handed George a small basket. "Empty your pockets into this basket and walk through again."

"Empty my pockets? Fraid not, Son. Not where I come from."

The guard looked George in the eye for the first time, seemingly speechless at the prospect that anyone would refuse.

"I'm not putting my personal stuff in that basket," George said. "What's in my pockets is *my* business, not yours."

"C'mon, George," Stuart pleaded. "It's to guard against hijackings."

"Hijackings?" George turned to the guard. "Son, I'm here to pick up my cousin from New Orleans. I ain't here to hijack no plane." George started through the doorframe again and the buzzer sounded, louder this time than the first, George thought.

Stuart caught him by the arm and tried to drag George back through the gate, but George stiffened to near immobility. "They check everyone, George. It's the law."

George stepped back through the frame, setting off the buzzer once more, and stood to the side, his arms folded. "Then I'll just wait right here."

Merle rolled her eyes and shook her head. "George, stop acting like a child. The plane's coming in any minute!"

Another person approached, placed a set of keys in the basket, and walked through the frame without buzzing.

"Wait just a damned minute here," George said.

"No metal in his pockets," the guard said.

The next person who approached had a suitcase, and she placed that plus her purse on a conveyor belt that went inside a box with an eye piece. The guard looked through the eyepiece for a moment, then the suitcase and purse came out the other side of the box. The woman stepped through the frame without buzzing.

"See?" Merle said. "That woman let them look in her purse *and* her suitcase."

"Don't blame me if she ain't got a sense of privacy."

"I'm going to the gate," Stuart said, starting to walk. Merle gave George a poisoned look and followed Stuart.

George thought about the things in the pockets of his overalls—his watch, his keys, his pipe cleaning instrument, and his pocket knife. He also had some coins, including three or four very old ones that he figured were worth something. There was his billfold. He sure as hell wasn't about to let anyone go rummaging through that and start making plans to rob him in that dark parking deck. Nor was he about to let them see his driver's license and learn exactly where he lived. He knew he was carrying a miniature screwdriver set, an Allen wrench, a metal tape measure, a cigarette lighter, some nails, his old badge from when he was on the volunteer fire department, and a metal shoe horn. He wasn't about to show that stuff to strangers and have them laugh at him for being a hick.

George wondered just what the guards would do if he went through the security frame and didn't stop when they hollered at him. He watched the guards out of the corner of his eye, and when he felt that they weren't watching, he edged around the frame and started up the concourse.

"Hey, you!"

George kept walking. In moments both guards grabbed him by the arms and marched him back behind the frame. George's face burned as he glared straight ahead. Every muscle in his body stiffened and his hard farmer's hands and arms ached to grab both guards by their collars and smash their heads together.

Two approaching passengers stared as the guards gave George

a firm, unnecessary shove, then turned back to inspect the alligator briefcases the two men carried. They passed through the frame as if the metal detector had been waiting for them all day.

*****

George retreated down the concourse out of the guards' sight. He looked at a sign that said Cocktail Lounge and wondered if he shouldn't wait there. George seldom drank, but right now he wanted to swallow half a bottle of whiskey and go back to tell the guards that he would arm wrestle them for the right to enter the gate area. He couldn't imagine either guard as much of an adversary, even though they were both at least twenty-five years younger than he. George knew his anger was capable of getting him in trouble at that moment. He'd never picked a fight, but he'd never backed down from one either. Since most of the trouble he'd witnessed in his life had arisen from someone else's stupid action, George usually withdrew from trouble, like a turtle sucking its head into its shell. He'd stayed on the farm rather than take a job in town so he would not have to deal with a boss. He'd stayed single so he wouldn't have to deal with the needs of a person more demanding than his iron-willed, self-sufficient mother. But these two young guards were questioning his manliness, and they might, before the afternoon was over, cause him to look like a fool in front of his cousin Jenna. As they'd already managed to do in front of Merle and Fat Stuart.

George recalled other struggles—when he'd faced down the power company when they tried to force him to let them cut a line trail through his property; when the farm equipment dealer in Augusta refused to honor the warranty on George's tractor; when the insurance company over in New Hampshire tried to raise George's rates because he didn't have lightning rods on his barn. George had won all those, and he planned to win the war against the metal detector, too.

When he took off his hat and scratched his tousled hair, it occurred to him that if the security machine could only detect the metal in his pockets, he could just place the contents of his pockets in his hat, then put the hat back on his head. That way the frame would not buzz.

George glanced up and down the lobby and began emptying his pockets into the hat. By the time the screwdrivers, the wrench, the keys and the shoe horn were in the hat, there was little room for his head, but he continued to fill the hat anyway—the coins and cigarette lighter, the wallet and watch and badge. He also found he was carrying a metal comb that he used to scrape ticks off his dog, and noticed that the frames of the reading glasses in his shirt pocket were also metal.

He tried to place the hat on his head, but two coins fell out. He took the hat off, retrieved the coins, then bent forward to place his head into the hat. When he was certain the hat would stay on his head, he began to walk slowly, carefully—graduation slow, he cautioned himself. A few articles settled around the sides of his skull.

Looking far down the concourse, beyond the frame where the security guards stood, George saw a small crowd forming. He assumed that a plane had landed. As he reached the metal detector, he felt the coins slip again. He stopped, waiting to see if anything might fall from the hat. George's eyes went automatically to the security guards, but they were watching the arriving passengers. George scanned the crowd for Merle or Stuart, but he saw no one he knew.

He took a step closer to the security gate and nothing moved, so he continued slowly. The first of the arriving passengers came through on the far side of the frame, where George had first tried to go before he was told about the security gate. George slowly turned his head the few centimeters he needed to see if any of the passengers were watching him as he crept toward the metal detector. In the distance, he now saw Merle and Stuart coming toward him. Merle was pointing at him, and George knew that his chances of getting through the gate were quickly vanishing.

George moved another slow step toward the metal detector frame. There was Jenna, all right, walking between Merle and Stuart. She looked stockier but not really fat, and her hair was still straight, although only shoulder-length, and gray, just as he'd imagined. Her permanent smile had planted deep crow's feet, and her unrelenting stare, without glasses, he noticed, seemed to drift by him. She'd obviously not seen him yet.

He was only one step away from the doorframe, and something, a coin or, perhaps, the shoehorn rested tenuously on the top of one ear. He kept his eyes on Jenna, still fifty feet away. That was when George noticed her stick, white with a red top, and saw the way she clung to Merle's arm. Merle and Stuart led Jenna around the metal detector gate toward George, who now stood stock still. Why hadn't they told him, George demanded with his silence as he glared. Merle made no sign, and Stuart just shrugged.

"Here he is," Merle said, barely audibly.

"Oh, Georrrrrrge . . . I hope you're not upset. I didn't want them to tell you what had happened so you wouldn't go feeling sorry for me before you could see that I'm doing just fine."

She hesitated a moment, then Jenna reached to hug George, but the slight motion of his head was just enough to bring the contents of his pockets spilling out of his hat. Jenna gave a little shriek but didn't move. Merle and Stuart watched as the coins and keys, shoehorn, tape measure and tools fell to the floor. Then the hat itself fell off George's head against Jenna's chest. She snatched it before it fell and held it against herself as an understanding smile slowly grew, and her cloudy eyes gazed past his head.

"George . . . I can only assume you have a *perfectly* good reason why you were carrying things on your head inside this hat?"

George's face burned, and he could barely speak. "Well . . . I guess not."

Her smile grew across her face as her eyes beamed more directly toward the sound of his voice. She began to laugh, her whole body shaking. Merle laughed, too, as did Stuart, who bent to pick up the spilled things from the floor. George, as always, refused to let himself laugh. But he did feel an odd comfort in those blank eyes that somehow glinted, quickly forgave his foolishness. Her smile, still perpetual, had lost its mocking quality.

George took the single small suitcase she carried. She thanked him. They began to move down the concourse back toward the parking deck, Jenna's hand firmly grasping his shirt sleeve.

"George," Jenna said, reaching for his arm. "This is just what I was most hoping for—you haven't changed the tiniest bit."

He looked over his shoulder once more at the security guards. Something told him to be relieved that he'd lost his opportunity to show those two that he'd figured out how to outsmart them. His mind struggled only for a moment, then Jenna squeezed his arm a little tighter, and George let the guards and his unfinished business go.

photo by Sylvia Martin

Fred Bonnie was born in Maine, in 1945. He graduated from the University of Vermont, fell in love with Southern writing while earning a degree in Chinese history, and moved to Alabama in 1974, where he worked as garden editor for Oxmoor House. From 1976 to 1979, he was garden editor for *Southern Living*. He has spent most of his last nineteen years as a freelance writer/photographer. Mr. Bonnie's stories have appeared in *Yankee, Confrontation, The Fiddlehead, Kansas Quarterly, Pacific Review* and other magazines and journals. He's published six books on gardening and an equal number of short story collections, this being his latest. He earned his MFA in Creative Writing from The University of Alabama in 1995. He presently lives in Winston-Salem, North Carolina, with his wife Rhonda Carter, who is an internal medicine resident at Wake Forest.